Shayne on the Dark Side

Michele stood before him.

He took out a cigarette and lit it without looking away from her. She picked up the negligee.

"Is that all you've got?" he said.

"I sleep in nothing. It's easier." She could tell from his eyes that they would make love. But she saw something else: that it would make no difference. If he felt it was necessary he would kill her.

Michele was right, but for the wrong reasons. The armed robber whom she'd just seen kill a cop with the same .45 now aimed at her was no ordinary thug—he was Mike Shayne. **And before the night was out, he was going to play a pivotal role in one of the biggest underworld drug scores ever!**

BRETT HALLIDAY

ARMED...
DANGEROUS...

A DELL BOOK

Published by
Dell Publishing Co., Inc.
1 Dag Hammarskjold Plaza
New York, New York 10017

Dell ® TM 681510, Dell Publishing Co., Inc.
Printed in the United States of America
Previous Dell Edition #0299
New Dell Edition
First printing—December 1974

ARMED...
DANGEROUS...

CHAPTER 1

The taxi pulled up in front of a big, blank-faced apartment complex on New York's upper West Side. The single passenger, a striking blond girl named Michele Guerin, leaned forward, puzzled by the reading on the meter.

She was wearing a beige suit, a good copy of an original from one of the Parisian dress houses, not much jewelry and little makeup. She was in her middle or late twenties. Her eyes were smoky blue and humorous, as if she considered her good looks and elegance a lucky accident which might just as well have happened to someone else.

"One dollar thirty," she said, too precisely. "I must give you one seventy-five. No?"

"OK," the driver said with a smile. "I'll let you get away with one seventy-five."

He took the two singles she handed him, made change, and leaned across to unlatch the door, a service New York taxi drivers don't do for everybody. He had been wondering about her. He couldn't quite fit her into any pigeonhole. Her accent was French, and her slowness in reading the meter probably meant that she hadn't been long in this country. Nevertheless, she had none of the earmarks of a tourist. He had checked her for rings. She was unmarried. Maybe a professional model, he thought, except that those girls tend to be skinny, and in her case there was no question at all that there was a real woman inside the expensive clothes. Another thing he had noticed about models—their expression was often vaguely dissatisfied and sulky, as though they didn't like having to show off clothes they couldn't afford to own. And there was nothing sulky about this girl's expression. An actress, he thought? But no, that didn't seem to fit either.

He watched her click up to the big glass double doors. She was just as attractive going as coming. He sighed heavily, a reasonably contented married man with three small children, put the cab in gear and drove away.

Michele could have stayed at a much sleeker apartment, at a more fashionable address on the other side of the Park, but she had liked the anonymity of this place, with no doorman or conciérge to notice when she came in or went out. One drawback was that she had to unlock the door herself, and after two weeks in New York she still didn't have the knack. While she was struggling, a man came in behind her and pressed one of the doorbells in the long double column.

"Hey," he said good-naturedly after watching her for a moment, "you've got it in upside down."

"I haven't!"

"Sure you have. Let an expert."

A voice spoke from the mouthpiece beside the bells. "Yes?"

"Jake Melnick," the man replied. "I've got a couple of stones I'd like to show you, Mr. Evans, if it's all right to come up."

"Why not?"

The buzzer unlocked the door. Melnick pushed it open with his foot, then took the girl's key, turned it right side up and slid it into the lock.

"The trick is, don't force it."

She smiled gratefully. "I am absolutely no good at machinery of any kind."

He gave her a speculative look. It was a familiar look to Michele, though she hadn't received it as often in this country as she did in her own. The men in New York, many of them, seemed to have other things on their minds. She measured Melnick with a quick appraising glance. He was carelessly, almost sloppily, dressed, which she knew by experience didn't mean he couldn't afford anything better. He was thin to the point of emaciation. A lighted cigarette dangled from his lips. There were amused lines around his eyes, cynical lines around his mouth, a combination that always interested Michele. Not that she had time to do anything about it now.

They skirted a sofa and a low ornamental barrier of rubber plants. The lobby was empty except for a man opening an envelope at the end of a bank of mailboxes. Smooth, characterless music came from hidden outlets in the walls. Michele was sure that no one ever actually heard this music, just as she hadn't ever seen anyone actually sitting on the lobby furniture.

An empty elevator was waiting. She pressed the button for the twelfth floor.

"I hear they give you a two-month concession when you sign a lease here," Melnick said. "The wife and I have been thinking about it. How is it, not too noisy?"

Before she could reply, the man at the mailboxes turned and entered the elevator with them. He captured her attention instantly, and the thought jumped into her mind that under the pretense of reading his mail, he had actually been waiting for them to appear. That was impossible, of course. He was tall and broad-shouldered. His rumpled gabardine jacket was unbuttoned and the knot of his necktie was loose. The tiny button of a hearing-aid showed in one ear. He was dark-haired and ruggedly built, and he moved with the lounging grace of a professional athlete in top condition.

"Aren't you in the diamond business?" he asked Melnick.

"Yeah," Melnick said, surprised.

"Jake Melnick, sure. Melnick and Melnick."

The door of the elevator closed, shutting them in. The big man glanced at the signal panel. There were eighteen floors in the building. A red light burned beside 12, Michele's floor.

"Which for you, Jake? Eight?"

"Listen," Melnick said, "I don't know you and I don't know what this is all about, but whoever you are—"

The car had barely got underway when the big man

threw the emergency switch. The brakes grabbed with a sudden violence that sent Michele back against the wall.

"Sure you know what it's all about," the big man said easily. "Larry Evans in 8-C wants to give a dame a diamond. If you waited till tomorrow somebody else might beat you to the sale."

"Let me out," Michele said urgently. "Please let me out."

"Keep in that corner, kid," the big man told her quietly, without taking his eyes off Melnick. "Nobody's going to get hurt but the insurance company. Now I show him the gun so he knows it's serious."

His big hand snaked under his left arm and came back with a heavy automatic. Michele's hands were pressed to her mouth. Please, no resistance, she begged Melnick silently. Do what he says. She was carrying quite a bit of money herself—he could have it and welcome. And when he was gone she would have to persuade Melnick to leave her out of it. She couldn't afford to be questioned by police. There might be photographers. This was fantastic! It couldn't be real.

The cigarette still dangled from Melnick's lower lip. It was trembling as his jaw trembled. He tried to say something.

"Wh-who—"

The big man gave a sudden barking laugh and looked at Michele for the first time. His eyes were hard and dangerous. A tiny reckless spark burned in each.

"I was calling somebody and they gave me a crossed line. How do you like that? The best tip I ever had, and it didn't cost me a cent."

Getting down to business abruptly, he let the ugly muzzle of the automatic give Melnick his orders. The frightened diamond dealer raised his arms and the big man touched his pockets from the outside. The wallet was in an inside jacket pocket, attached by a short length of fine chain to a heavier chain around Melnick's body. The big man jerked at it angrily, bringing Melnick up on his toes.

"Cautious bastard."

He took up hard on the chain, twisting the diamond dealer against the wall. He laid the taut chain across the metal hand-rail and brought the butt end of the .45 down smartly. A link broke and the wallet came free.

"Now let's see how much cash you're carrying, Jake."

The diamond dealer fumbled out a smaller wallet. "One of those stones," he said weakly, "I didn't insure it yet. I'll give you a better price than the fence would."

"Sure, sure, send me a check. Let's have the watch."

Melnick stripped off his gold wristwatch. The bandit dropped it into his side pocket. Giving no warning, he stepped in close against Melnick and slammed him in the stomach with a fist the size of a small ham. Melnick caved forward, making a sound like a popping balloon. He grabbed out at the big man to keep from falling. For an instant they were in a kind of clumsy embrace, and all Michele could see was the diamond dealer's hands and wrists. The big man pushed him away with a vicious low-voiced obscenity and, as he fell, chopped at his head with the butt of his .45.

Melnick pitched to the floor. The big man whirled on Michele. She shrank back.

"Any remarks, baby?" he said savagely.

"No," she said in a weak voice, and thrust her purse toward him.

The left side of his mouth and his left eye worked in a convulsive half-wink, half-twitch. It frightened her. She could see that he was on the verge of going out of control. "I have money," she faltered.

He ripped the purse out of her hands. She knew exactly how much she was carrying—eight hundred and three dollars, eight hundred of it in new fifties and hundreds. It put him in a better humor.

"Green," he observed. "My favorite color."

He took her watch and a bracelet. After dropping them in his pocket with the rest of the loot, he threw the emergency switch back on and pressed the lobby button. The car continued upward. Its electronic brain had been told to take them to the twelfth floor, and it had to clear that out of its memory before it could start down. He watched the lights, his head on one side as though with the help of the hearing-aid he could listen to his own thoughts.

"You will let me get off?" she said. "Please, I am French. I go home in two days' time. I can prove this to you. I can show you my passport. If I should talk to the police about this I would miss my plane. That is not my desire."

The car stopped at 12. She made a slight movement and he snapped, "Stay where you are."

The door opened and closed. She said in a small voice, "It is true, you know."

His eyes jumped to the lights. The car was slowing for an unexpected stop at nine. He moved over into the door-way. The door slid back to show an overweight lady in an elaborate hat.

He said brusquely, "We've had an accident. Next car."

Her coquettish smile vanished as she looked down. Melnick's long legs had jackknifed under him, and he looked as though he had been flung down violently from a great height. One entire side of his face was covered with blood. The woman's mouth came open. The bandit stabbed angrily at the Close button, and the door obeyed him.

He made a scornful noise. "Give the lady some smelling salts. Now relax. I hardly ever smack a doll with a .45 when we haven't been introduced. I've got to dump this bastard. Then I'll tell you what I want you to do. Just do me one favor, and maybe you'll catch your plane."

"Yes," she breathed.

"I may have picked up a tail. I had that feeling. Let's not hurry walking out of here. Like we're husband and wife and I'm taking you to dinner. We'll walk over to Central Park West and pick up a cab. I'll let you get out after a couple of blocks, and you can forget the whole thing."

"All right, I shall try."

"Do better than try, baby. That's the best advice I can give you."

The little giveaway muscle was jumping again in his cheek. They were passing the fourth floor. He punched for

12

three, and when the car stopped he looked out carefully, then dragged the unconscious man to the corridor. Melnick's arms and legs seemed totally uncoordinated, as though they were fastened to his body with cotter pins. She found herself thinking, oddly, of a line from *Macbeth,* a play she had studied in her last year at the *lycée:* "Who would have thought the old man had so much blood in him?" Melnick's face was so bloody that it might have been flayed. His clothes were sodden. He groaned heavily as the man responsible for his wound kicked his foot out of the doorway so the door would close.

Michele was sorry, but someone else would have to find him. As soon as she was released she meant to hide in the nearest movie, coming back only after all the excitement had died down.

As the car slowed, approaching the lobby, the big man gripped her arm above the elbow and moved her to face the door. She tried to force a smile.

"You don't have to smile," he told her. "We've been married a long time."

"That hurts."

"Too bad."

The door opened and he walked her out into the lobby. She was surprised to hear the hidden musicians still picking away at the same Rodgers and Hammerstein number. All her plans had been turned upside down in the time it took a dance orchestra to play thirty-two bars. Thank God there was no one in sight. Then her breath caught. There was movement behind them and a voice called suddenly, "Mc-Quade!"

The big man turned, keeping his hold on Michele's arm. The man who had come out from behind the second bank of mailboxes was short and pugnacious-looking. He needed a shave and he seemed very tired. His eyes were bloodshot.

"Where've you been keeping yourself, Mac?" he said.

"Wrong number," the big man said, his voice easy and unflurried. Michele felt the tension in his grip. "My name's Carl Williams."

"Like hell your name is Carl Williams, honey," the short man said. "It's been a couple of years, but I don't forget faces that easy. I do forget what we had you down for. A payroll in Brooklyn, wasn't it? About seventy-five G's?"

"You are drunk!" Michele said sharply.

"I'm a little drunk," the detective agreed. "But then I'm off duty so it's OK. What I like to do is knock back a few and then ride the subways looking at faces. When I spot one that's familiar I follow the guy, like I followed Mac here. It's kind of a hobby."

He started toward them. "And who are you, sweetheart?" he said to Michele. "Mrs. Carl Williams or Mrs. Francis X. McQuade?"

An elevator arrived behind him and let off the plump lady in the big flowered hat. Seeing the tense little tableau she stopped short. Her eyes, Michele noted incongruously, were the pale blue of souring milk. Her mouth opened and the scream she had swallowed upstairs came out, with plenty of pressure behind it. The detective looked away from McQuade for only an instant, but when he looked back the .45 had appeared in McQuade's big hand.

The detective congealed, both hands well forward. His tired look was gone.

"I see I made a mistake," he said. "You don't look anything like McQuade. And even if you did, nobody was killed in that stickup, so God bless you. Take off. Till we meet again."

The scream from the woman at the elevators rose in pitch until it cut out abruptly as she dropped to the floor in a faint. McQuade and Michele still had fifteen or twenty feet to travel to the door, and they didn't hurry. The detective remained fixed, as though he found himself playing the child's game of statues, and would have to pay a forfeit if he was seen to move. But he was tense and ready. He wouldn't have been a detective without a gun inside his coat. McQuade had pulled Michele in against him so she partially screened his body, but would the detective let that stand in his way when the shooting started? Michele knew better.

McQuade said softly in her ear, "When we get to the door I'm putting a slug in his knee. After that you're on your own. If you ever see me again, start running."

She was breathing in quick shuddering gulps. McQuade stopped with a muttered obscenity. Something on the other side of the front window pulled at Michele's eye. Luck had been fairly good to her lately, but now it had turned on her with bared teeth. A uniformed policeman was making out a summons for a car too close to a fire hydrant. His horse looked in at Michele.

McQuade could handle one armed man, but hardly two. He hesitated. The momentary stitch in his concentration gave the off-duty detective his chance. He broke for a low sofa, reaching for his gun. McQuade fired. The recoil of the heavy automatic against her side almost twisted Michele out of his grasp. The detective landed on the nubbly carpet with a strange little moan, and grabbed at his thigh. McQuade took a half step toward him, tightened his hold on the struggling girl and fired again. The impact of the heavy slug flipped the detective over.

One of the potted rubber plants rocked crazily and fell, spilling dirt on the carpet. The big scalloped leaves camouflaged the upper part of the detective's body. Something about the angle and position of his feet told Michele that he was dead.

CHAPTER 2

McQuade came around fast, in a half crouch. Michele's shoulder was against his chest, and she felt the heavy thump of his heartbeat. Through the front window she caught a flash of the mounted policeman's face. The horse, too, had twitched around, startled by the shots.

McQuade ran for the elevators, dragging Michele with him. The plump lady had fallen on her back, her tight skirt riding up to show the underpinnings of her girdle. McQuade propelled Michele into the elevator and heaved the unconscious woman out of the doorway. He jabbed the button for the basement.

"Please let me go now," Michele said. "You think if you hold me in front of you the police will not shoot. No, no, you are mistaken."

He said nothing. When they reached the basement he walked her out into a cement-block corridor which came to a dead end to the right of the elevators. In the other direction two workmen were trying to ease an upright piano, riding on a dolly, into the freight elevator. The corner of the dolly had caught on the door, and until the workmen could back it off there was no way to get by.

McQuade yanked Michele back into the elevator and pressed the button for the twelfth floor.

"Twelve," she said. "We are going to my—"

"Shut up."

He watched the lights, his gun ready. If they stopped at the lobby there would be more shooting. They went by without stopping and he released her at last.

"An off-duty cop on the subway!" he said in disgust.

"Eight million people in New York, and I had to get on the one train with that guy. You know I don't have a single conviction? I mean that. Not even for carrying a weapon. And now all of a sudden the breaks start going the other way." He appealed to her, as though he really wanted an opinion. "Why did those bastards have to be down there with that goddamn piano?"

She was watching him carefully. The corner of his mouth was working again. His eyes darted from side to side.

"Every cop on the West Side of Manhattan is going to be trying to ream my ass in another couple of minutes."

Michele forced herself to breathe normally. She must think. After being shot once, the detective in the lobby had been no further threat to McQuade. McQuade had shot him a second time because he had been recognized and called by name. One more killing now would make no difference. She would stay alive as long as she could make herself useful, and no longer.

"What's the apartment number?"

"Twelve H."

"Who lives there besides you?"

"No one. I am alone."

He gave her a quick glance, and she explained, "I am here on business. It is a colleague's apartment, so I need not stay in hotels. He is in Los Angeles."

"What kind of business?"

"Clothes."

They reached the twelfth floor. McQuade punched the buttons of two higher floors so the car would continue without them. He took her arm again in his punishing grip.

"Don't, please. This is not necessary. There is no place to run."

His upper lip lifted. "Nobody tells me what to do. Remember that, kid."

She took him down the short hall. There were two locks, the regular spring lock, which even an amateur could open with a strip of celluloid, the other a heavy bolt which couldn't be forced without special tools. As usual, she tried the wrong key first.

"For Christ's sake," he snapped, shouldering her aside. "Don't take all day."

After throwing the bolt he took her arm again, nudged the door open, stepped quickly inside and kicked it shut.

They were in a large one-room apartment. It was comfortably furnished, though the furniture looked as though it had been ordered by phone. There were no books, no pictures on the walls. There was a kitchen area to the left, a bathroom to the right. Without relinquishing his hold on her arm, he looked into the bathroom and took her to the big windows.

"We are really alone," she said. "You can release me now."

With his free hand he lowered the venetian blinds and adjusted the slats so he could look out without being seen. The three buildings in the group, tall, unadorned rectangular slabs, were arranged in U-shape around a paved court which was black with parked cars.

A siren sounded.

"There they are," he said, sounding almost pleased.

He released her arm. She rubbed the place, hoping she would live long enough to see it turn black and blue.

"Do you want a drink? There is bourbon. Gin, perhaps."

He rubbed his knuckles along his jaw. "Give me a slug of bourbon."

She went to the little refrigerator. He bolted the front door and put the key in his pocket. Then he picked up her bag, unzipped it and shook out its contents on a low coffee table. While Michele waited for the water to run warm, she watched him. He picked her car keys out of the litter, two keys chained to a plastic tag with a New York number and the Chevrolet insignia. He weighed the keys for an instant before setting them aside. Then he looked at her passport. After checking the statistics on the first page —none of them, as it happened, true—he flicked past the intervening visas to get the date of her entrance into the country.

He looked up suddenly. Their eyes met and held. His stare was colder than the ice cubes in her hands. Michele shivered. She had to come up with something fast.

He swept everything off the table into his cupped hand, keeping out only the car keys, and returned it to her bag. When she came in with the drinks she found him studying the diamonds he had taken from Jake Melnick in the elevator. There were four unset stones, each wrapped separately in a fold of tissue paper.

"The transaction is profitable?" she said.

"Fair."

He refolded the tissue around the diamonds and transferred them to his own wallet. She handed him a glass filled with whiskey and ice.

"Please, may I say something?"

He cut her short. "Shut up a minute."

He took a long taste of the whiskey. As if to comment on his situation, another siren began to howl. It was coming across the park, coming fast. His face worked.

"I should have stopped on the way up to clobber that bastard Melnick. I mean *clobber* him. As soon as he comes out of it they'll have my description."

"If he recovers at all," she said.

"Hell, I barely tapped him, I'm sorry to say." He came to his feet suddenly, then waved it away. "Too late. But I don't know what's wrong with me. Why didn't I think of it?"

They were silent for a moment, listening to the sirens. He looked at her over the raised glass.

"You begin to get the idea, baby."

"I think so," she said quietly. "I do exactly what you say, or I stay in America, in an American graveyard."

"Baby," he said with one of his disconcerting returns to good humor, "there wouldn't be enough left of you to bury." He drank, watching her. "Are you expecting anybody?"

"No, no one."

"Then let's get organized. The first thing they'll do is go through the building." He slid the clip out of his .45 and added two loose rounds from his coat pocket. "How much of a look did that cop get at you? I mean the cop out on the street."

"I think he did not really see me."

"He saw you, but how much did he see? Now when they knock on the door"—he moved to the bathroom, his gun still in his hand—"I'm going to be inside here. With the light out. And I'll be watching you, kid. I can't hear out of one ear, but there's nothing wrong with my eyesight. Don't try to give him any message, because the minute that cop puts one foot inside the room—"

"I understand you, believe me."

He finished his drink in a long swallow and went to the kitchenette, where he poured himself another, larger than the first. Glass in hand, he kept moving around restlessly, as though something about the apartment bothered him. He opened the closet and looked in at her clothes. She had only brought three suitcases from Paris. He went for his hat, which he had dropped on the table by the door, and put it out of sight in the closet.

"You can use my car," she said, "or if you like I will drive you. Then you can have the car. By the time the police are told it is stolen, two weeks will be gone. Three weeks, four, whatever you say."

He turned and watched her, but it seemed to her that he was listening to something else.

"I know," she said. "How can you believe me? I know your name but I have no intention of telling the police. This is not my affair. My passport has been forged, you see. That will be a difficult thing to prove to you, but I believe I can do it if you will listen to me. Please listen, for the love of God."

"Put something else on," he said. "The cop saw that suit. And that jerk Melnick—as soon as he can talk he's going to mention the twelfth floor. Put on a wrapper or something. Some goddamn curlers in your hair."

She gave an elegant half shrug. "You heard nothing that I said."

"Later," he said impatiently.

She stood up. "Must I really put in curlers?"

He grunted. "You look too good the way you are. That's what they'll remember. I want you to look like a slob."

She made a little grimace, her eyebrows going up. She took a negligee out of the closet and started for the bathroom. "Curlers. Very well. But when you see me next, you will be sorry."

"Huh-uh," McQuade said, shaking his head.

She stopped. "What does that mean?"

"I want you out where I can see you. You might decide to wave a towel out the bathroom window."

"I do not wish to be a heroine. I wish to exist."

"Get it through your head, kid: *I'm taking no chances.* When a cop's involved they still use the chair in this state." He snapped his fingers. "Get into action."

She gave another tiny shrug, using her eyebrows as much as her shoulders. "Michele," she told herself aloud, "do as he says."

Tossing the negligee on the sofa, she unfastened her earrings and put them on the coffee table beside the keys to the Chevrolet. She unfastened the inner catch of her suit jacket and shrugged it off. She was wearing a half-slip and a low-cut bra. The bra was nothing but crossed ribbons and two fragments of transparent fabric.

She was reasonably objective about herself, she believed. She knew she had faults, some of them severe, but they were mainly of a moral nature. Physically she was satisfied with the way she looked. Her breasts she knew to be excellent, though they were the despair of her dressmaker, who liked his clients to look like slender young boys. Reaching behind her, she unfastened the little double hook and the bra fell to the floor.

She was facing McQuade. He watched her, his head lowered. She continued to undress, without self-consciousness or coquetry, trying to hold his eyes so she could judge his reaction. She could not make mistakes. If she misjudged him to the slightest degree, she was finished. So far he was a puzzle to her. When he moved, with the power and grace and some of the sullenness of a big cat, he gave off a kind of electricity that agitated her nerve ends and left her feeling charged and unsure of herself. He was attractive, certainly, one of the most attractive men she had encountered in a long time. If she had met him casually she would have made no attempt to look beneath the surface, for it wouldn't have mattered. She would have put him down as a handsome animal who might or might not be worth a little attention, depending on her schedule at the time. Life had taught her one big lesson—never to commit herself to anyone. The only person she could be completely certain of was herself. And now with McQuade, she had to make up her mind what steps to take, how best to reach him, then back her judgment to the limit. She had seen that he could think and act quickly, but how good would a story have to be to fool him? In Michele's view, anybody who chose to make his living as an armed robber had to be a little stupid. There were easier and safer and more satisfying ways of earning money. And there were moments when he seemed stupid, or at least not interested in making the necessary connections. But she had the nagging feeling that this was a manner, a style which he had decided to affect because he considered it suitable to his profession.

Now she stood before him naked.

Her dressmaker, poor darling, would have been appalled, but she could see that McQuade found nothing wrong with her appearance. His mouth was no longer taut at the corners. He took out a cigarette and lit it, all without looking away from her. Perhaps, after all, she thought, things were going to be all right. She picked up the negligee.

"Is that all you've got?" he said.

"To sleep in? I sleep in nothing. It is easier."

She drew on the negligee. It had no fastenings except the belt at the waist. She cinched it in tightly. She could tell from his eyes that they would have sex, probably soon. But

22

she saw something else: it made no difference. If he felt it was necessary he would still kill her.

The phone rang. He did not jump; he had good nerves, she noticed. But the flesh around his eyes contracted. There was no question about it. Big and handsome he undoubtedly was, but when he wanted to he could look very mean.

The phone rang again. He motioned to her and she picked it up.

"Hello."

"Michele," a man's voice said. "What progress?"

"Ah, *chéri*," she said. "I wished for you to call. For tonight I fear I must beg off. The noise, the rushing about, it has given me a headache. I must go to bed with my bottle of aspirin."

"Anything wrong?" the voice said quickly. "If there is I can send somebody. Say yes or no."

"No. Call me tomorrow. But I am truly sorry. It came on all at once, like the ceiling falling."

"You know, of course, that there isn't much time."

"I think of nothing else. But it will arrange itself. Now I must hang up. Forgive me. My head."

She put the phone back. "A man I met," she said quickly. "I said perhaps I could take dinner with him. Now what are you thinking, with that face like a hurricane? That he will come to see if I am with another man? If he does, shoot him."

He held her eyes a moment longer. "Don't try to pull anything." He drank. "Come on, put that junk in your hair."

"You won't like the way I look, believe me, like the Statue of Liberty." With her drink, she made believe she was holding a torch. "No," she suggested, "why not wash it instead? That would be better."

She watched him thinking about it. "OK. Wait a minute. You still look like something in a magazine."

There was an open box of powder on the chest of drawers. He spilled some of it down the front of the negligee. Then, with the burning end of his cigarette, he put a hole

23

in a conspicuous place. The negligee had cost her seventy-five dollars at a Fifth Avenue store, a fact it would have been unwise to mention.

"And more lipstick," he said. "Really smear it on. You've been hitting the bottle all day. You're so plastered you can't walk straight."

"Plastered? Oh, I see. Drunk. It will be difficult. I have never felt less so."

She unscrewed her lipstick and took it to the bathroom mirror while he watched critically from the doorway.

"Put it on crooked."

She bore down heavily on one side. The lipstick slipped and left a red smear on her chin. By the time she was finished she had changed her appearance very much for the worse.

"Plastered," she said darkly, eyeing her reflection. "Now I am repulsive enough?"

"Get to work on your hair."

He stayed in the doorway while she washed and rinsed her hair. She was toweling it briskly when the doorbell chimed.

McQuade moved quickly. The .45 was back in his hand, and he used it to motion her out of the bathroom. She twisted the towel around her head with one deft motion. He passed her the key, which she had to have to throw the bolt. Before opening the one-way peephole, she looked back at the bathroom. McQuade let the .45 come into sight for an instant and pulled it back. It was a reminder she didn't need.

She turned. She could use this interruption, she thought, to prove to McQuade that she had no intention of betraying him. With her back to the bathroom she twitched the negligee open so the nipple of one breast showed. She looked through the peephole. The policeman outside was young, callow. Having heard the clink, he was looking straight at the peephole.

"Police officer."

She threw the bolt. Steadying the turban with one hand she opened the door.

"How nice, a policeman," she said loosely.

He glanced down at her disordered negligee. His glance lingered for an instant on her breast. Incredible, she thought. I have shocked him.

"Sorry, lady, but we're making a check. There's been some trouble downstairs. How long have you been home?"

"Hours. I have been washing my hair." She smiled lopsidedly. "What trouble?"

The policeman licked his lips. "Well, a shooting."

"That is how it always is!" she cried. "When anything exciting happens, I am washing my hair!"

"What have you got here, just the one room?"

He looked past her. His eye stopped on her clothes, which still lay in a heap on the floor, and jumped back to pick up the whiskey bottle and glass.

"I am terribly messy," she murmured.

She gave him another bleary smile and started to close the door. He put his fingers against it from the outside. He glanced down the corridor.

"Searching the building, for God's sake," he said. "When you shoot a cop you don't hang around to see what's going to happen. You get away fast. Frankly, I could use a drink."

He grinned. Michele let her smile fade.

"What is this, please?"

He took his hand off the door. "Nothing! Now don't get your bowels in an uproar. I just thought, seeing you're all by yourself—"

"A policeman!" she cried. "And you are supposed to protect us! Trying to force your way in with some nonsense about a shooting!"

She whipped the soggy towel off her head and slapped him with it. He retreated, his arms up to ward off another blow.

"OK, OK."

"It is very much *not* OK!"

She banged the door shut and turned the key. McQuade came out of the bathroom grinning. The mask of outraged indignation stayed on her face for another instant, and then she smiled. They met in silence, coming together hard. She felt a moment's alarm, as though she found herself at the top of a steep hill in a racing car without brakes. Then her mouth opened to his kiss.

CHAPTER 3

The apartment was dark.

Michele twisted, coming to one elbow. They were together on the sofa. Without much effort, by releasing a
catch and making a few other minor arrangements, they
could have opened the sofa into a double bed. But they
hadn't taken the time.

She reached across to the lamp. "Fair warning. I am
turning on the light."

She snapped it on and found McQuade studying her sober-
ly, one arm behind his head. He was naked to the waist.
His .45 was wedged behind the cushions. He had placed it
there with one hand while caressing her with the other.
During the lovemaking that followed she was fairly sure—
not completely sure, because for a time things were rather
turbulent and confused—that he never for a moment forgot the pistol. She was anything but foolhardy. Under no
possible circumstances would she have tried to seize it, but
he had given her no chance. On the whole she liked people
who showed that kind of common sense.

She ran the palm of her hand along his arm. "I love the
way you feel," she said.

He had said nothing since she slapped the policeman
with the towel. With the tip of a finger she traced the lines
on his face. He was not her type, of course. She had a favorite restaurant in Paris, which served indifferent food
with tremendous style, at a fantastic price. She could never
take him there. He would make the place and the other
people in it look foolish.

Suddenly, looking into his eyes, she had the answer to

the puzzle. They were both in trouble! They had to work together! It was obvious, it would solve everything. All she had to do was sell it to him.

She kissed him lightly. "I must do something about this lipstick."

"Who cares?"

"I care, my dear."

She left him on the sofa and looked at herself in the mirror over the bureau. She groaned. Her hair!

She did what she could. Still naked, she went for drinks and cigarettes, then told him to hold still while she wiped some of the lipstick off his face.

Finally he sat up. She gave him a cigarette and lit it for him. He filled his lungs with smoke and breathed it out slowly.

"Yeah," he said.

And that, it seemed, was to be his only remark on what had happened.

He swung his long legs off the sofa and pulled on his shirt. He fitted the button of his hearing-aid into his ear and dropped the battery case into his shirt pocket. She poured whiskey into a glass for him without ice.

"Somehow," she said, "all at once I find it extraordinarily difficult to remember your name."

"It'll come back."

"No, when I washed my hair I washed it out of my brain." She laughed. "No, perhaps you are right. Names are easy to forget only when they are not important."

She drank, while the laughter faded out of her eyes. "I think you are not much of a sentimental person, my friend. This encounter was pleasant, exciting perhaps, but it has no bearing on what you must do now."

She pulled his hand so the back of his wrist touched her breast. Holding his hand in both of hers, she moved it slightly. The little friction made her shiver.

"You will stay with me tonight. I think you will stay awake drinking and making love as often as it pleases you, and all the time you will be thinking of your problem.

What will you do with me? I am a girl who knows your name, who saw you shoot a detective."

He stirred and she said quickly, "I am putting myself in your head, wondering what lies I must tell you to make you let me go. And I can think of none. What I must do, then, is simple—tell the truth."

"Don't go that far," he said. "You might bust something."

"No, I have just realized that I can help you. How hard will it be to place those diamonds, for example?"

He grunted. "Not easy."

"Did you really find out about Melnick from a mistake on the telephone?"

"Hell, no. I didn't want him to wonder about it. I had a tip from a guy in his workroom."

"And perhaps he will think of that person, and then if the police are clever they can get your name."

He shot her a sharp look, took his hand away from her breast and drank slowly.

She went on, "The thing for you to do, my dear, is take an airplane to some distant country, where the jewelers will not ask you if anyone was killed because of these diamonds. To do that you will need money. You will need a passport. I will get you both. All you must do for me in return is touch me lovingly from time to time, and help in a little adventure of my own."

"Don't try to con me, baby," he said harshly. "I'm in no mood."

"To be specific: fifteen thousand dollars. Half to be paid tomorrow, half the day after. An airplane to Portugal. Meanwhile, concealment."

"And what do you want me to do, knock over a bank?"

"Not a bank, darling," she said seriously. "Say you will consider and I tell you."

"At your service," he said humorously.

"It is real, I assure you. We plan to steal a truck. It will be escorted by two armed policemen. At the most, three. But there will be five of you, and with luck there will be no shooting."

He gave a quick cough of laughter. "You can do better than that. Take your time. We've got all night."

"Apparently you do not believe me?"

"I don't believe in Santa Claus, either. You're mixed up in something, that much I'll give you. Nobody carries eight hundred bucks in cash without a reason. And there was something off about that phone call. But a heist?" he said scornfully. "You? Stealing a truck? How dumb do you think I am?"

Turning, he put his hand against her bare stomach. She sucked in her breath and her breasts rose toward him. A tingling started in odd places, including the soles of her feet.

"I wouldn't knock you off, baby," he said. "Let's stick together till your plane goes. Of course, I know you can always fly back, or call the cops long distance. But I'll be out of sight by that time. It's OK."

He was smiling slightly, making no real effort to make it sound convincing. She tried to ignore the little tinglings he had started.

"Listen to me—"

"Where have you got the Chevy, downstairs?"

"Yes, where the cars are parked. Darling, you must listen to me for one minute."

But he had tuned her out, as though by switching off the battery in his shirt pocket. He took the wallet out of his hip pocket and counted the money he had taken from Melnick, frowning. She could see that he didn't consider it enough.

"Wait a bit longer," she said. "Then there is a way I can convince you. I will take you to a place to meet the others. Can you lose anything by finding out? Naturally I do not make a habit of stealing trucks. It is new in my experience. But this is a special truck. It carries a valuable cargo. I made a plan, secured a backer, hired a person to recruit others. They will carry it out. I myself risk little. If it fails, I return to France no worse off than before."

At last she had his attention. She continued: "During these two weeks, you understand, I am not in New York. I am visiting friends near Nice. Anyone who says I am in New York is a liar."

"Who rented this apartment?"

"Someone with no idea at all that it is being used at present. I rented the car myself, using my passport. As I told you before you decided to listen, the passport is in the name of an imaginary person."

He poured himself more whiskey, turning over what she had said. "So if anything goes wrong, you'll be drinking rum punches on a beach in France someplace."

"That is why I am willing to pay fifteen thousand dollars for thirty minutes' work. But nothing will go wrong."

He snorted. "With five people things are bound to go wrong. Look at what happened tonight. A simple little stickup, with automatic elevators and no doorman. So I had to get on a subway train with the one son of a bitch in New York who would recognize me. A traffic cop had to be tagging a car outside the front door for a parking violation. A couple of delivery jerks had to bring in a piano at half past five in the afternoon. A piano! That's three things that couldn't happen again in a hundred years, and they all happened inside of an hour."

"Granted. But let us be very very careful and we can lengthen the odds. If you are interested, and I think to be realistic you have to be interested, I will go over the plan and let you suggest improvements."

"What do you mean, to be realistic? I don't need anybody. I never have."

She put her hand on his. "All I want you to do is think about it."

"What's in the truck?" he said after a moment.

She could see that he was half-persuaded, but she could not risk stepping on some hidden prejudice. "That, I am afraid, is none of your business."

His eyebrows came together. She decided it was time for a flare of temper of her own. "Truly! Put yourself in my situation. There are things I must reserve. A truck, X, will proceed along a certain street, Y. Why should it matter to you what is in it?"

He gave a grudging grunt. "What looks really fishy—two days before something like this you don't start looking for an extra man."

"How very true," she said dryly. "Before I left France I was given the name of a person to approach. He was said to be excellent. I could tell him how many others I wanted, with what specialties, and he would find them for me. He did this. But he is a man with one fault—he becomes quarrelsome when drinking. Never mind, no one is perfect. And he is no longer one of us. He is in jail, awaiting trial for fighting in a bar. A person of no consequence was injured. We have been wondering—can we do it with four? The answer is yes, but with danger. The plan was for five. And now suddenly here you are, perfect for it! You have reasons to be careful, you will not become drunk in a bar. On top of all your other qualities"—she smiled—"you make love marvelously."

He came close to returning the smile. "It wasn't too bad. Where have you got these guys?"

"One is a girl. When everything becomes quiet I take you there."

He took an ice cube in his mouth along with the bourbon and crunched it between his powerful jaws. "I don't say I like it," he said. "I've always been one man. Even that can get complicated, but bring in five people and everything's multiplied. I'll look it over. It could be an out. I don't say it is. It could be. Just don't try to maneuver me, that's all."

Reaching out suddenly, he took the back of her neck in a powerful grip. She went with the pressure, knowing that for the moment she had nothing to fear.

"Because what have I got to lose?" he said in a tone that was almost tender. He released her and continued, "If you want to back out of that story, do it now. This guy who got pulled in for brawling, so you'd have a spot open—that's too damn convenient."

"Convenient or not, it happened."

"OK, it happened. Now what about Portugal? Why Portugal?"

"Because that is where the plane goes. Darling, one step at a time. Meet these people, let us tell you more about what we plan. Sometime tomorrow we will go over the actual ground. You will agree that it can work. If I have told you a single lie so far, one, you may put your revolver to my head and pull the trigger. We must wait here some hours. There is more whiskey. There is the television. Perhaps there is a program you wish to watch, unless you have a better idea of how to use the time."

He gave her a penetrating look under lowered brows. "I hope this is on the level, kid. I wouldn't want anything to happen to you."

She shivered slightly, and the shiver set the tingling going again. She shouldn't let him affect her this much. It was out of proportion. She was a cool, self-possessed girl who knew what was important and what was not important. She had plans for the future. He was a gunman, a killer. If she had to take him to Portugal, never mind, she would drop him in a hurry once she arrived. But why had nobody, out of all the people who had made love to her, ever made her react in just this way?

"Damn you, are you going to kiss me?" she said.

CHAPTER 4

From the basement corridor, they went up a short ramp to the delivery entrance. Even after several hours together, he still trusted her exactly as much as before, which was to say, not at all. The back door was unguarded. Keeping a firm grip on her arm, he took her to her parked convertible. There was no activity anywhere in the parking area. He wedged his big frame into the cramped space behind the front seat. He had his gun out, and he made sure that she saw him press the muzzle against the back of the driver's seat. She nodded. To signal a policeman and try to jump from a moving automobile was hardly her type of thing, gun or no gun.

She covered him with a robe. After turning on the lights and starting the motor, she reported in a conversational tone, "No sign of anybody."

She cramped her wheels and eased out of the parking slot. A police car was parked outside on Central Park West. She kept her eyes straight ahead as she passed, and then watched the mirror. The police car stayed where it was.

"I think we are OK," she said after several blocks. "In a moment I start into the park."

A red light stopped her at Eighty-sixth Street. When the light changed, she blinked for a left turn and plunged into Central Park. There was no one behind her.

"Now come up to breathe, darling."

McQuade emerged. Putting his gun away, he swung over into the front seat, where he forced a pocket comb through his rough black hair.

"Would you like to drive?" she asked innocently. "No, you wish to watch me, not the road. I think you still do not altogether trust me."

"No, I do not altogether trust you," he said in a parody of her accent.

She continued east. After leaving Central Park she headed for the entrance to the Franklin D. Roosevelt Drive. This took them downtown. They crossed the river on the Manhattan Bridge. From there it was all expressways. After crossing the Verrazzano-Narrows Bridge to Staten Island she left the Staten Island Expressway at the third interchange and headed north toward St. George. McQuade, she noticed, was watching the turns closely. To prove to herself that she was no longer worried about his gun, she made several unnecessary twisting detours.

"Are you sure you know what you're doing?" he said suspiciously.

"Certainly. I have been congratulated on my exquisite sense of direction. Here we are, then, in the wilds of Staten Island, and I think it is safe to tell you something more about what is to happen. It is to take place in Manhattan, the day after tomorrow. On Sixth Avenue, at the corner of Twenty-seventh Street. A boy named Billy, who is clever with machines, will change the stoplight at that corner so it can be worked by a small button. Very well. The truck approaches. The light turns. We then create a small disturbance, a diversion, so two of you, you and Billy, will have no difficulty getting into the truck to drive it away. The traffic goes in one direction only on the cross streets. You will go the wrong way. We will arrange matters so the street will be clear. Then a warehouse, where the truck is unloaded. You drive a few more blocks, leave the motor running and walk away. After that, Portugal."

"You're leaving some big gaps."

"But naturally. Before it happens in real life, we go over it many, many times."

"What kind of truck, or is that one of the things you want to keep from me?"

"A sanitation truck, my dear. I have a uniform which I

35

hope will fit you. And I think we must borrow one of those trucks tomorrow so you will know exactly what to push and what to pull."

"No problem," McQuade growled. "I was driving heavy equipment before you started going out with boys."

"This is better and better. One of my people says he has experience driving trucks, but I have been doubtful. He is something of a boaster."

"Fine. Just what we need."

"He was hired to use a gun. Actually he shoots well. This I have seen."

"That's the ticket—shoot a few more cops, make ourselves popular."

She glanced at him. "It may be necessary, you know. But only if you must."

"Jesus! For a garbage truck!"

She gave a mocking laugh. "Later I will tell you what kind of garbage. On the plane, perhaps—yes, on the plane. We turn in ahead here. Someone should be watching the driveway."

A stone wall, six feet high, topped with splinters of glass in cement, ran along one side of the road. Presently Michele turned through a gap where there had once been a gate; only the hinges remained. As she came to a halt, the beam of a three-cell flashlight darted out of the underbrush and hit her in the eyes.

"Hi," a voice said after a moment.

A boy of eighteen or nineteen, in a short-sleeved sports shirt and tight white levis, came out near the front fender. He was carrying a shotgun as well as the flashlight.

"We thought you'd be here earlier, Michele. I'll call the house and tell them it's you."

"Billy, here is a new man. His name is Frank. He knows how to drive a truck, among other things."

"Hey!" the boy said. "That takes a weight off. My opinion of Spaghetti, he's ninety percent mouth. If he can get into one of those trucks, sight unseen, and not do something wrong, so can my aged grandmother."

He pointed the long flashlight past Michele. McQuade

stared back into the beam, his eyes slitted. "Well, hi," Billy said approvingly.

After the flashlight turned away McQuade said, "Now let's see you, kid."

The boy turned the light on himself, holding it directly beneath his chin. This threw grotesque shadows across the upper part of his face. To distort his appearance further, he goggled his eyes and grinned idiotically.

"What, me worry?"

Michele laughed. "Ring them up, Billy, and come with us. We can show Frank the plan quicker than tell him."

"I want to see Spaghetti's face when you say he's not driving. He's been going around like a four-star general."

Billy crouched beside an Army field telephone and cranked it twice. When he had an answer he said simply, "Michele."

After ringing off, he rigged an electric eye to point across the gap at knee level. He came around to the door on McQuade's side.

"If there's room."

McQuade moved. The driveway was lined on both sides with fine maples, the space between them choked with underbrush. The roadbed needed maintenance, and the Chevy scraped its oil pan once or twice, though Michele drove slowly. The house was a quarter of a mile away, a great rambling structure, topped with gables and cupolas and ornamented with scrollwork, in the style of the 1890's.

Michele parked at the foot of the front steps. As they crossed the wide porch, a girl inside began to scream.

Michele had been under tension for the last few hours, and her heart gave a sudden jump. *Now* what? Couldn't she leave these miserable creatures alone for two minutes?

"Think you can tease me, you white bitch?" a man shouted hoarsely.

"Don't! You can't make me!"

"Oh, yes, I can make you. Yes, indeed. What I'm going to do to you, honey, I'm going to lay you six different ways and you're going to love every minute!"

McQuade pulled away from Michele's hand and leaped toward the front doorway.

"Get it through your head!" the man inside shouted. "You're going to ——"

McQuade saw a heavy-set, burly Negro mauling a young white girl with a dense mop of black hair. He pulled the Negro into a right-handed punch that traveled less than a foot and lifted him clear off the floor. The little splat as fist and jaw collided sounded like an egg being dropped.

"Stop it, both of you!" Michele cried.

Her cry went unnoticed. A second man appeared in the archway at the end of the living room. He was smaller than McQuade, with snapping black eyes, a thin two-part mustache and slicked-back hair. He was wheeling a dress rack, a simple contraption of iron pipes running on rubber-tired wheels. A dozen or so identical dresses in plastic bags hung from the central pipe.

He looked from McQuade to Michele, his eyes jumping like furtive animals. He whirled the rack around and thrust it at McQuade.

The Negro landed on the worn carpet with a crash that must have startled the termites in the old beams. McQuade batted at the dresses with both hands. He tried to sidestep, but the smaller man kept pushing the rack at him, keeping him off balance.

Michele cried, "Ziggy, that is truly *enough!*"

McQuade took a backward step and finally got a grip on one of the uprights. He braced himself. The rack reversed and the smaller man began to retreat. On the floor, the Negro shook his head and gathered himself. Michele stooped beside him and said something urgently, in her agitation speaking in French. He brushed her aside and began to get to his feet, trouble written all over his black face.

"Brownie, you fool, stand still and listen!"

Billy, the boy who had met them at the gate, hurled himself on McQuade from behind. McQuade twitched violently and brought his elbow back into the boy's midsection. Billy went flying, an anguished look on his face.

The Negro, coming up, dealt McQuade a powerful blow

38

in the kidneys. McQuade spun around and the dress rack went careening away, carrying its manipulator ahead of it. In front of the fireplace, he tripped on a low table and went down. The rack came down on top of him.

The girl, a skinny thing under her wild crown of black hair, grabbed McQuade's waist and hung on grimly. McQuade chopped at the Negro's head, and caught him on the ear with a swinging right that took him out of contention again. McQuade turned to meet Billy as he came at him swinging a poker. He went in underneath the poker and caught it as it came down. He twisted, yanking hard. The poker whirled away.

The dress-rack man had untangled himself, but he kept clear of McQuade until the Negro recovered and could come at him again. Then he darted in with a karate chop which McQuade caught on the side of his head. A swinging backhand blow sent Dress Rack reeling. A fat Tiffany glass lamp with a beaded shade fell to the floor.

The skinny girl finally succeeded in working one leg between McQuade's. The Negro grabbed from one side while Billy leaped on him from the other, and they all four went down, in a flailing, churning knot. Dress Rack moved around the little group with the marble lamp base, waiting to get a shot at the big man's head.

Michele continued to scream at these impossible Americans to act like civilized people. But suddenly the whole thing struck her as less awful than funny. She collapsed laughing into a tall chair. It was wild, high laughter, and after an instant it reached the struggling group on the floor. Dress Rack peered around in alarm, and lowered the lamp base. The Negro looked up, and McQuade hung a solid right high on his cheekbone.

That was the last blow struck by either side. No one could go on battling in the same room with that cascade of laughter. The skinny girl freed herself, smiling, and came to her feet. Her blouse was in tatters and one strap of her bra had torn loose, but the bra didn't have much to keep under restraint. Billy, sitting back on his heels, began to grin. In a moment he was hooting as hysterically as Michele.

The Negro, dazed, was flickering in and out of consciousness, but his lips, too, began to move. Only Dress Rack still looked mad.

"Put it down, Ziggy," Michele sputtered. "I told you. Did I not tell you? Do you remember? I told you it had to work. And the dress rack. You see what a weapon? What you can do with it?"

"I never said you couldn't," Dress Rack said stiffly.

McQuade came heavily to his feet. "What are we doing, playing games?" he said, massaging his knuckles.

Michele's laughter was nearly under control. Catching Billy's eyes as she started to speak, she was off again.

"Oh!" she gasped finally. "My poor ribs. Brownie, are you all right?"

The Negro waggled his jaw. "If someone will pass me the bottle of Scotch. Who is this gentleman?"

"His name is Frank. He is taking Tug's place. And this is Brownie." She pointed. "And Irene. And Szigetti, sometimes called Spaghetti. I spoke of a small disturbance we mean to create on Sixth Avenue." She spread her hands. *"Violà! This is it!"*

McQuade touched the side of his face and looked at his hand. There was blood on it. Szigetti, smoothing his mustache with quick flicks of his thumbnail, studied McQuade closely.

"I've run into you somewhere," he said.

"Have you?" McQuade said.

"In Florida or someplace?"

McQuade looked at him with more interest. "I've been in Florida."

"Yeah," Szigetti said, studying the bigger man speculatively. He turned to Michele. "We were counting on taking Tug's split and divvying it up. We were working on the new timing when you came in. My principle is, the fewer the better."

There was no sign of merriment in her face now. He said quickly, "I'm not griping! I'm no complainer, anybody can tell you that. I thought we could see how it shaped up with just the four of us. And if you still thought you needed the extra man, I had somebody to suggest. A kid I can vouch for over the years, and you could get him for a fraction of what Tug was getting."

"Did you approach him?" she said sharply.

"No, no, not without getting a go-ahead from you. But I happen to know he's available."

"You can forget it, Ziggy. Frank, that blood on your face, do something about it. We don't want to call attention to you with a bandage."

"It's not my blood," he said.

Brown had picked himself up and was pouring himself a slug of good Scotch. "You're welcome to it, baby," he said softly. "For now."

"Now will everybody please stop this?" Michele said. "It was a stupid mix-up, and all my fault. We are going to be friends for thirty-six hours, because we can do this only if we work together. After that you may fight with knives or guns or anything you please."

"Blade work?" Brown said blandly. "Not for me. I'm a nonviolent cat. First thing I'm going to do is buy a red Thunderbird and some new threads. Then I'll accept bids from the chicks."

"Where's the bathroom?" McQuade said.

Michele said, "Show him, Billy."

Billy took him out through a large dining room. The table was littered with aluminum trays, the remains of four TV dinners. He opened the door of a washroom off the kitchen.

"There's a tub upstairs," Billy said, "and it's about three and a half feet long. You couldn't get in without a shoehorn, Frank."

"Yeah?"

The boy looked down diffidently, then up into Mc-Quade's eyes. "That was some fight," he said, and added, "Paper towels is all there is."

McQuade grunted. Inside the washroom, he closed and locked the door.

Instantly his manner changed. He listened. When he heard Billy's retreating footsteps he turned on the hot-water faucet. The water was rusty. Leaving the water running, he raised the lower half of a narrow frosted window and looked out. Then he eased his big frame through the opening and dropped to the ground.

He moved cautiously around the house. The living-room windows were open. He dropped to his heels to listen to Szigetti's overly emphatic voice.

"All I'm saying is I *saw* him somewhere. And he's got the wrong smell. I just want to make sure you know for a fact he's OK."

"I do know that for a fact," Michele said coldly. "He has the wrong smell because you want another one-fifth added to your price."

"No! I was just checking up. If you say he's OK, he's OK. In this kind of situation, I like to trust the guy on the right of me as well as the guy on my left, and the way this Frank McQuade strikes me, he strikes me as being maybe a little too independent."

"He is independent," she conceded, "but I have a lever to use on him. He will give us no trouble."

"I'm glad to hear that," Szigetti said, too heartily. "One other thing. There can't only be one guy in charge. Tug— he was a natural, we're all his boys. Now I know the setup, the kids have confidence in me. I'm the logical man. I'm not bucking for anything, understand, but if everybody feels—"

McQuade's lips shaped a savage smile. He slipped away without waiting to hear more.

He had already spotted the telephone wire. He dropped to his hands and found the lead-in box, just above the masonry of the foundation. He pried the box open with a small screwdriver, working by feel. He struck a light, snapping the lighter shut again almost at once. He did something inside the box, closed it carefully and backed away, paying out a thin copper wire. At intervals, he pulled it taut and tacked it against the underside of a clapboard.

He swung back into the washroom, bringing the wire with him. He took out his hearing-aid battery case and opened it. Where the batteries should have been there was a neat arrangement of printed circuits and transistors. He loosened a terminal and tied in the wire. After checking the button in his ear, he closed a gap in one of the printed circuits with the point of his screwdriver. He turned on both faucets in the wash basin and sloshed the water around with one hand. In a low voice, speaking directly into the battery case, he gave a Manhattan number.

He waited impatiently. Then, in the same low urgent tone, he said, "Power? This is Michael Shayne. I'm in."

CHAPTER 5

It had started two days earlier in Miami, when Michael Shayne, the big, hard-driving, redheaded private detective, received a phone call from his friend Will Gentry, Chief of Miami Police.

Gentry wanted to know if he was busy. Shayne looked across his cognac at his secretary, Lucy Hamilton, who was sitting on the sofa where he had left her. He said yes. Gentry said in that case he would put it another way. Could Shayne, as a small return for all the favors Gentry had done for him over the years, interrupt what he was doing and get his ass over to the St. Albans Hotel in Miami Beach on the double? Shayne sighed. He told Lucy he was sorry as hell, and put on his shoes.

He met his old friend in a room on the tenth floor of the hotel. A tired-looking man with a square, rugged face shook hands with him and looked at him searchingly.

Gentry said, "This is Inspector Power from New York, Mike. Sanford Power. I've known him since he was a pup. The way it is now with these goddam jets, we're getting to be practically a suburb of New York. If Sandy and I didn't work together, we'd hardly ever catch anybody."

Gentry was red-faced and sad-eyed, a courageous, honest cop who was also one of the finest persons the redheaded detective knew. At the moment he was smiling too effusively, like a used-car salesman in bad need of the commission.

"He wants to borrow you for a week, Mike. Sit down and he'll tell you about it."

Shayne said dryly, "I don't think I'm going to like this."

He waved away the chair he was offered, reversed a straight chair and swung a long leg over the seat. "But you put it so nicely, I'll have to hear about it before I say no."

Gentry's too-anxious smile faded. "I was hoping you wouldn't take your usual hard-nosed attitude, Mike. This could be one of the biggest things in years."

"For me or for you or for New York?" Shayne inquired. "Go ahead, Inspector. But I have to warn you—there's a sign on my office door that says, 'On Vacation.'"

"This wouldn't be much of a vacation," Power admitted, rubbing his eyes. "And I hope you'll call me Sandy instead of Inspector. I'm a long way out of my jurisdiction. Nobody knows that better than I do."

"Then if this isn't official," Shayne said, "offer me a drink."

"I'm sorry!" Power said. "This thing has been hammering at me. I don't know if I'm coming or going. I'm a beer man myself, but Will told me what you like."

He opened a bottle of Hennessey's. There was a brief interruption while the drinks were poured.

He resumed abruptly, "There may be a certain amount of money for you, Mike, somewhere between thirty and sixty thousand. There's also a certain amount of danger. And there's one other thing Will tells me not to stress, but from my point of view it looms pretty large. We have a chance here of crippling the international drug traffic, and it isn't a chance that's likely to come again."

"Every time somebody seizes a few hundred pounds of heroin they say they've crippled the drug traffic," Shayne said. "It still seems to go on."

Power winced. "I've been guilty of that kind of statement once or twice myself. But this is different. It isn't a few crummy pushers or wholesalers. It's the men who put up the money, and by money I don't mean a few thousand dollars. I mean approximately two and a half million."

Shayne looked up sharply. "I've never heard of professionals handling a shipment that large."

"The circumstances are unusual," Power said in the same

dry tone Shayne had used. "Do you want to say no at this point, or listen to some more?"

Shayne drank some cognac and chased it with a sip of chilled water. "You mentioned a certain amount of danger and a fairly sizable fee. I take it the two things go together?"

"That's correct. The two and a half million is a retail valuation. A cash equivalent on the primary level would be in the neighborhood of half a million. A ten percent payout would be a justifiable figure for information leading to the apprehension and conviction of et cetera. As far as danger goes, with the right kind of preparation I think it can be minimized. This is very much an undercover assignment. I can't risk using anybody from New York, even if I had anybody who could do it, and quite frankly, I haven't. I drink a brew or two with Will whenever I'm in town, and I've heard about a few of your exploits, Mike. I think you can handle this job. I'll go further—I think you may be the one man in the country who can handle it."

"Good God, Will," Shayne burst out angrily. "I can see you at these beer-drinking sessions. A cop blows in from the big city, and you think you have to impress him with all the crime we have down here."

"I didn't exaggerate," Gentry said. "And you're not just a local man anymore, Mike, I might point out. You've been known to make the New York papers."

"And since when did you start believing what you read in the papers?" Shayne made a disgusted face. "And where would this undercover work take place, in southern Florida, where I know my way around, or in New York, where I have to ask directions to find the Latin Quarter?"

"In New York," Power said. "That's not necessarily a disadvantage. You're listening, and that's a start. I've been in police work all my life, Mike, a small matter of forty-three years. This is easily the biggest thing I've ever come within shouting distance of. Bear that in mind. And I want you to face the fact that if you get out of this room without saying yes, you'll have to come up with some damned good reasons. Being on vacation is not a good reason."

"That was mainly my secretary's idea," the detective

said impatiently. "I suggest we get on with it."

"Right," Power said briskly. "Bear with me, Will. There's going to be some repetition. This is the basic situation."

He tasted his beer. "It starts in a poppy field in Burma or eastern Turkey, and ends up on West One Hundredth Street in Manhattan. Ninety-nine times out of a hundred we can't break into the chain any higher than the next to the last link. If not the user, the pusher, the man who supplies him, who's usually also a user himself. Sometimes the customs people pick up a batch as it comes in, but one of the facts we have to deal with is that most of that information comes anonymously from inside, as a cheap way of getting rid of somebody who's stepped out of line. Nobody has to tell me none of this does much permanent good. I'm not fooling myself. It's a war, Mike, and in a war you do what you can. You don't turn down a shot at an enemy tank because a couple hundred others are over the hill, and what's one out of a couple of hundred? But I didn't come down here to sing the 'Star Spangled Banner.' "

He reached abstractedly for his beer, and shook it to start the bubbles. "There's a law against using or peddling, and you do your best to enforce that law. You can't make an arrest without evidence. You see somebody who's well known to be a junkie. He's obviously on the nod, with a fresh needle mark on his arm. That's not enough. You have to catch him with the needle, with the actual drugs. Sometimes you get lucky, and you're on the spot when he makes his connection. You put your evidence in a manila envelope, and when you come into court you damn well better bring that envelope or they throw you out on your ear. Well, this happens three or four thousand times a year in greater New York, so naturally we've worked up a pretty solid routine. We can usually put our hands on those envelopes. Even after we get a conviction, if we get a conviction, we still hang onto them because the case may go up on appeal, or it may be reopened by a higher court ruling on something else. But a time comes when there's no point in holding onto the evidence any longer, so what do we do?

We burn it. This happens once every two or three years. We go through the property vaults, sort out the dead envelopes and truck them up to the Department of Sanitation incinerator on West Fifty-sixth Street. And it all goes up in smoke. Sometimes there's a story in the papers about it, and even if there's not, the news gets around. For a few days all the junkies in New York are very depressed."

He had finally succeeded in catching Shayne's interest. The redhead sat forward and said thoughtfully, "Two and a half million bucks worth of junk is a lot of junk."

"About two tons," Power said. He took a card out of his pocket. "Here are the figures for the last time. Total value $3,548,000. The heroin alone was $2.7 million. The rest was cocaine, marijuana, goof balls, odds and ends. Total number of arrests, eleven thousand over a three-year period. This time we're cleaning house after two years, but the retail price has gone up. We'll have an exact total later. Two and a half million is only a guess."

"Give or take a million, still it's something to shoot at," Shayne said. "And negotiable, as good as cash. But I don't see your problem. How many cops do you have in New York? About twenty thousand. You ought to be able to move two tons of junk across town without being hit."

"Now wait. Who thought the Japanese would hit Pearl Harbor? Who expected anybody to rob the Brink's warehouse? That's the point. They can assume we won't expect anything, because who in God's name would have the gall? The stuff is downtown now, and our security is good there. Nobody's going to walk in with a few handguns and walk out again alive. The incinerator at the other end is built like a fortress. We'll have a bunch of people there to certify that the right envelopes are burned. That means the attempt has to take place between those two points. We'll be out in the open for forty-five minutes and you know we won't use twenty thousand cops. In the ordinary course of events, two would be enough."

"Nobody would try it without some good information," Shayne said slowly.

"Apparently they have it. I have an idea where it comes

from, but never mind that now. Let him go on dreaming."

"What I'd do," Gentry said. "It's like any narcotics action—something has to happen before you make an arrest. But hell. Use twenty or thirty plainclothesmen in unmarked cars. Land on them the minute they make their move. You'd have a nice pinch."

"That was our first idea, Will. But listen."

He heaved up out of the chair and began to pace. "This is no nickel-and-dime operation, two or three crazy amateurs shooting for a big score. A couple of tons of narcotics—you need an organization to market it. Maybe *the* organization. And if you want to find guys who are willing to take on two armed cops in city traffic, you have to spend some money. You'll need a minimum of six people. Three or four vehicles. Maybe a hundred thousand dollars. I don't want to pull in the small fry this time. I want the man or the men who hired them, who can always hire somebody else. And this time, damn it, I have a chance! I used to be in charge of Narcotics. I inherited the usual complement of stoolies, and I developed some of my own. About three weeks ago I began to get indications that something big was in the offing. A gun named Tug Wynanski turned down a job for a certain date, and that was the same day we'd reserved time at the incinerator. I hate to use shoo-flies, but sometimes you have to. I put men on every clerk in the property department, and seventy-two hours later I had the leak. We watched him around the clock. We put men on Wynanski. For a week now I've known exactly how many people are in it. I have their names and records. They're holed up in a rented house on Staten Island, which I have under surveillance. How many times has it happened in your experience, Will, that you know in advance that a crime's going to be committed, who's going to commit it, and where you can put your finger on them whenever you like? As far as I'm concerned, it's never happened!"

"If your surveillance is that good," Gentry put in, "you should be able to tie in the higher-ups without using Mike. No?"

"Not unless I let them pull off the heist exactly as planned. That gets *too* risky. If we lost track of them somewhere along the line, I'd have some serious explaining to do to the Super."

He took a quick pull at his beer. "Wynanski's been tagged once or twice, always for small things. What he's supposed to be good at is putting together a package. You bring him an idea and he handles the details. There's one trouble with him, he has a temper and he likes to drink. He drives over to Manhattan every day, and on the way back to Staten Island he's likely to stop at a bar. Here's how I think we can get Mike in. Two days before D-day, we'll pick up Wynanski for assault. They'll believe it. He's the main guy on the execution level. It'll leave a large hole."

Shayne snorted. "You're out of your mind. What do I do, knock on the door and say I've heard on the grapevine that they need a man?"

"What I haven't told you yet is that there's a girl, a French girl named Michele Guerin. She's the one who's been handing out the advances. She has an apartment in Manhattan. According to her dossier, it's her first time in this country, and she probably has the usual foreigner's idea of how much everyday violence there is on the streets of New York. Now imagine this scene. She's driving down Fifth. Shots are fired. A big redhaired hoodlum—no, we better dye your hair, Mike, that thatch of yours is too well known—not a red-haired hood, a *black*-haired hood, backs out of a bank with a gun in his hand. He shoots an off-duty detective and commandeers the girl's car. Why wouldn't she fall for it? She saw it happen."

Gentry said, "One thing I don't like about that idea. It's too public. Too many things to go wrong. Because what if Mike runs into a *real* off-duty detective, shooting real bullets? How would you time it so the car would be there at the right moment, and then wouldn't get jammed up in traffic? I think it ought to be inside. You'd have more control."

Shayne looked at his friend in amazement. "Will, do you mean he's already sold you on this pipe dream?"

Gentry's eyes moved uneasily. "It sounds far-fetched the first time you hear it, Michael, but it takes hold. It could be worked. The way I see it, it's in an elevator. No problem about the timing—you simply wait till the girl shows up. You only need two men. Your straight man comes in with her. Mike's waiting. All three of them get in the elevator. If somebody else gets in, no matter. Mike pulls his gun. The straight man—say he's a gambler, carrying a real roll. Mike has to slug him. He can use the old cackle-bladder routine from the con games—a plastic membrane filled with chicken blood. He has it in the palm of his hand, and claps himself on the forehead and all at once starts bleeding like a damn pig. *Then* Mike shoots the off-duty detective, on the way out. He grabs the girl and backs into the elevator and lays up in her apartment. A few prowl cars circulate around with their sirens going. That's all the atmosphere you'll need. The girl needs somebody like Mike. She offers him the job. Why not? We can think of a few refinements, but basically it's all right there."

Shayne shook his head morosely. "How many beers had you put away before I got here?"

"Quite a few," Gentry said, "and every time I have one more it looks a little better. Where's the hole in it, Mike? All we want to do is establish you as a gunman in trouble, and it shouldn't be hard. She won't know you're shooting blanks." Suddenly he smiled broadly. "Sandy, show Mike the picture of this doll in a bikini. He'll stop arguing."

Shayne said impatiently, "If she looks that good in a bathing suit, aren't there any easier ways she can make money?"

"She's definitely not routine," Power said, "but none of the rest of this is, either. I'll tell you what Interpol has on her. She's thirty-two, and well preserved. For three years, maybe longer, she was the mistress of a Greek shipowner. She went along on yacht trips with some highly placed people. She spends money freely. They think she carried some stolen bonds from Paris to Macao a year ago. She was suspected of blackmailing the younger son of a minor king, and that's all, except for one small fact. During the bond investigation an agent heard her phoning somebody named

Adam." He looked at Gentry. "Does that name mean anthing to you, Will?"

Gentry shook his head. Power went on, "It meant something to me, and it meant something to the agent who put it in the dossier. Actually we know quite a bit about the man, considering that we don't know if Adam is a first or a last name. He's English, probably not by birth. What we all agree on is the nature of his business. He finances the international movement of guns, drugs, gold, stolen paintings—you name it. He may or may not use an actual bank, nobody knows. We don't know if he's one man or a group. We don't know where his headquarters is. It could even be some kind of a code name, though that I really do doubt. Well, I haven't put away quite enough beer to give you my lecture on international underworld finance, and I don't know such a hell of a lot about the subject anyway. But if you're in the legitimate export-import business, shipping goods from one currency system to another, you need a legitimate banking connection. And if you're in a *crooked* export-import business, you need a crooked connection."

Shayne shrugged. "You'd do better to take this to the FBI. Everybody there has to be either a lawyer or an accountant."

"That's not what I need," Power told him. "I need somebody to get this girl's confidence. I ought to mention that when she isn't working, she seems to prefer large, rugged men."

"Which is why you thought of Mike," Gentry said gravely.

"Hell, we need everything going for us we can get."

"Christ!" Shayne said.

Power opened a folder on the bureau and handed the detective a six-by-eight glossy photograph of a girl in a two-piece bathing suit, standing in a stiff breeze on the bow of a sail boat. Shayne studied it for a moment.

"About the fee," he said, "I'll want that in writing."

Power laughed. "You can have it in writing. I had a feeling you'd like her looks. Now how could a lovely girl like that get involved in something like this?" He picked up his beer again and looked into it as though if he stared hard enough a scene would take shape. "I think they were sitting around somewhere in the south of France, she and our Mr. X—Adam something or something Adam. He mentioned a proposition he'd heard about in New York. A hundred-thousand-dollar investment, a couple of million in return. And what a coup for their side! The poor underpaid cops worked and slaved for two long years, picking up a dribble of heroin here and a dribble of marijuana there, and then they lose it all in one afternoon. He's toying with the idea, but he can't use any of his regular connections in the business because he's afraid they'll throw it away. And the girl, who's tired of running penny-ante errands, says, 'Let me!' Adam likes to work with gorgeous girls, it's one of his trademarks. He gives her the name of a New York gun, Tug Wynanski, who will do all the donkey work. Now cops always go by likelihood and percentages. How many cops would believe this girl was the contact on a big-time stickup? I'm retiring next year, Mike. This would make a nice thing to retire on. Listen—even if you can't get anything conclusive on him, find out his name! Blow his anonymity and he's more or less through. Sure, somebody else will come along six months later, but that's the condition of police work. It goes on."

Shayne poured himself some more cognac. Both men watched him.

"And what if I do succeed in getting in without getting myself killed? I'll be at the bottom. How do I find out anything about this banker you don't already know?"

"We can bypass the girl. Say they have a series of ten steps. You carry out the first nine, and then pull a fast switch that puts you in possession, you personally. Then you can make him come to you. That's only the outline. It needs a lot of work."

"I'll say it needs work," Shayne said. "What do you think about it, Will?"

Gentry said impassively, "I wouldn't have asked you over if I didn't think you could swing it, Mike. You'll be in touch with Sandy all along, and he'll have his men within shouting distance. There's a risk, but maybe it's no worse than some of the jams you get into under your own steam. You know what I think about the heroin business. I think everything about it stinks."

"If you want to stop it," Shayne said evenly, "all you have to do is change the law."

"Mike, I know you think doctors ought to handle the problem instead of cops, and it could be I agree with you. But that's not in the cards right now and you know it. Personally I don't like the idea of these creeps thinking they can make monkeys out of the New York police. My God, if anything went wrong no cop anywhere could show his face in public for weeks."

Shayne thought about it while he finished his drink, balancing inevitable dangers against possible results. It was wild and improbable; common sense told him that the odds against coming to grips with the shadowy banker were very long. But Shayne had always done his best work against the odds, and he found himself calculating how much luck he would need to bring it off.

"I just hope they don't ask me the way to the Empire State Building," he said, and reached for the phone. "I'll see if Tim Rourke can talk his paper into giving him a few days off on speculation. He's a born ham. Nothing he'd like better than hitting himself in the face with a cackle bladder."

CHAPTER 6

In the washroom in the eerie Victorian house on Staten Island, Shayne unfastened the wire from his battery case after reporting in to Inspector Power, opened the window and tacked the wire to the outer sill. Then he washed his face in rusty water. Dying his hair and eyebrows had changed his appearance more than he had thought possible. Everything had gone as Power had predicted until the moment when Szigetti said he thought he had seen Shayne somewhere.

Quickly Shayne reviewed what he knew about Szigetti. Power had had little information about the man. His arrest record was short and unimportant. He had been a Marine for four years. He had been court-martialed for selling supplies but acquitted for lack of evidence. His discharge had been honorable.

A transistor radio, tuned to a disc-jockey program, was playing when Shayne entered the living room. Irene danced toward him with thin arms extended. He embraced her. Without a partner, her entire skinny body had been in active motion, but this was not Shayne's style of dancing at all.

"You're creaky, Dad," she said.

Shayne let her go with a disgusted wave. "Where do they keep the liquor?"

She tried to hold him. "I didn't mean anything. I like to dance that cornball way. It's a change."

"I want a drink. Where's Billy? He'll dance with you."

"He had to go back on guard. And who's going to drive in here in the middle of the night? I mean, it's nuts."

55

"There you are," Shayne said, spotting a bottle. "I don't suppose we have ice."

"Sure we have ice."

She went to the kitchen. Shayne emptied somebody else's watery drink out of a jelly glass and filled it from a bottle of blended rye. Irene came back with a handful of ice cubes.

"Where did Michele find you, anyway?" she said, putting one in his glass. "I really thought we were raided when you walked in."

"I like to see a girl put up a fight," Shayne said irritably.

She laughed. "It only took five of us to slow you down. You know what I was thinking when I had you around the waist?"

"Don't tell me."

She was standing close to him, drinking. She was older than he had thought at first—twenty, perhaps. Her torn blouse was held together with a straight pin. There was a prominent horizontal bone at the top of her ribcage. Her skinniness was charged with vitality, like a naked wire. Her hair was long and messy, and not much face showed. From across the room she had merely looked eccentric, but at a distance of less than a foot she was an arresting and unsettling girl. She idly slid her fingertips inside the waistband of his pants and gave him a small tug.

"Later?" she said.

"Who knows?"

"Not that it matters," she said, "except to me, but I had an off-Broadway part last year. Just a walk-on. You didn't see it—it only lasted nineteen performances. That's the way I look at this—a part. But *God*, I'm nervous."

She touched the outside of his jacket, feeling the hard bulge of his .45. "I had a vague suspicion."

Across the room, Michele was talking to Szigetti, her eyes on Shayne. Brownie was slumped in a leather-covered Morris chair, his dark face as uncommunicative as a wall. All were holding drinks. Shayne walked over to Michele and asked if there were any cigarettes.

"You have some, Ziggy," she said.

He unwillingly offered his pack to Shayne. "I was just saying," he said. "Basically the idea is good, but I got a couple of minor suggestions. The one thing I don't want to touch is that act of Irene's. The big black buck and the Greenwich Village beatnik. That's going over big."

Shayne looked down bleakly. "Do you and Brownie get the same cut?"

Szigetti's eyes jumped away from Shayne, not quite reaching the Negro, who regarded them impassively.

"As far as that goes."

"Then let's have less of this color crap," Shayne said.

Szigetti looked at Michele for support. "What did I say wrong?" he asked on a high note.

"We change the subject," she said firmly. "I have told Frank about your shooting. Perhaps you will show him the gallery."

"Well," Szigetti said grudgingly, "I've been sopping up booze all day. I could be a little off."

He finished his drink and started for the kitchen, saying carelessly, "Brownie, let's do some shooting."

Without change of expression, the big Negro followed. Only Irene stayed upstairs.

"Exhibitionist," she said with a look at Szigetti's back.

The others, waving cobwebs out of their eyes, went single file down a narrow flight of steps to the basement. It was a spooky place, lit only by two dim bulbs. Rust had eaten holes in the furnace, but the bin beyond was still half-filled with dusty coal.

Szigetti faced into the shadows. "What's the matter with that light down there? See if it's loose or what, will you, Brownie?"

Brownie sloped off, keeping his head low to avoid the obstructions on the ceiling. A bright light came on, showing a pocked target nailed to a plywood panel. The distance, Shayne judged, was about twenty-five yards.

"Be careful," Michele told Szigetti.

He squinted at the target, holding a short-barreled .38 loosely at his side. "I won't plug anybody." He risked a quick look at Shayne. "They knew how to build houses in the old days. I had Billy stand halfway to the road while I did some shooting, and he thought it was crickets, for Christ's sake."

Brownie called, "OK?"

"OK."

Brownie was concealed from view behind a hot-water tank. Suddenly a beer can flew into the light. Szigetti fired, sending the can spinning back with a clank against the masonry wall.

"You bastard," he said, laughing. "You almost tricked me that time."

Suddenly a rat scuttled across the concrete floor, heading straight at them. Michele screamed and seized Shayne's arm. A shot from Szigetti's .38 checked the rat briefly, knocking it off stride, but it kept coming. Michele tightened her grip convulsively and went on screaming as the rat scuttled up to her feet. It had been put together out of brown cloth and darning thread, and stuffed with cotton. At close range it didn't look much like a rat. Some of the cotton stuck out through the rip made by the bullet.

"Ziggy, you monster," she said, her hand to her breast.

"And I don't know what angle it's coming from," Szigetti said, pleased. "That's the beauty of it. Depends on what string he pulls."

While he was talking, a cardboard head poked out abruptly from behind the water tank, disappearing the same instant that Szigetti fired.

"Missed!" Brownie called. He added in a lower voice, "No, you didn't. Nicked his ear."

Szigetti gave a complacent laugh. "Take a shot," he told Shayne. "I noticed you carry a .45. A .45 slug would really blow a hole in that rat."

Shayne's .45, of course, was loaded with blanks, which made a noise but wouldn't knock any stuffing out of a stuffed rat. "No, thanks," he said. "I stopped practicing years ago."

"Go ahead," Szigetti urged him. "Take a couple of cracks at the target anyway, if the rat scares you. I'd like to see what you've got in the way of a draw."

Shayne smiled. "What are we doing, rehearsing for television? No, you're too hot for me, Szigetti. After that much sauce I might not even hit the target."

Szigetti sneered. Suddenly Shayne said, "Now I know where I saw you. You were in the Corps."

The other man looked at him with slow surprise and put away his .38. "Four long years. What outfit?"

"I was a D.I. at Parris Island," Shayne said. "I forget what year you were there."

When Szigetti told him, Shayne said, "The mustache makes the difference. I keep running into guys, but it always takes a minute. After the first half-dozen cycles all the boots begin to look alike."

Szigetti, in good humor again, thought this called for a drink. They trooped back upstairs and finished the bottle. Another bottle appeared, the same harsh blend, Shayne was sorry to see. Szigetti was no less ready to reminisce than any other former Marine, and he stayed in a good mood as long as the others were willing to listen. All his officers, for one reason or another, had had it in for him, but just the same, he had generally managed to fix their wagon.

When Billy was called in off guard, he suggested a game of poker. Michele had never played, but she was willing to learn. She sat beside Shayne, her knee touching his leg. Between them, they collected most of the money at the table. Szigetti believed himself to be an expert but lost steadily. He crouched suspiciously over his cards, smoldering.

"Of all the goddamned luck!" he said, slamming down aces and queens after Shayne took the last pot with a low flush.

"Luck?" Brownie said. "That's poker-playing, man."

Michele stood up quickly and told Shayne to come with her while she found him a place to sleep.

"I know what," Irene put in from across the table. "No, that would be immoral."

Shayne gave her a half shrug and followed the French girl.

"You can use Tug's room," Michele said when they

were upstairs. "A toothbrush and so forth will have to wait till tomorrow."

She turned on the overhead light in an empty bedroom. There was a mattress and pillow on the big iron bedstead, but only one rumpled sheet.

"Primitive," she admitted, "but can you manage for two nights?"

"It's better than jail," Shayne said. "No women in jails."

She listened at the door, then closed it and came into Shayne's arms. She kissed him hungrily.

"I would love to stay with you," she whispered. "But Ziggy is so wild, it would make him worse. Tomorrow we make love. Do not forget. I take you to New York. When we are alone, let me suggest ways, darling."

Shayne's role didn't require him to make an answer. His arms tightened and he let one hand slide down her back. She broke away.

"Tomorrow will be a sensational success, I promise you. Even better will be the day after, then the day after that. Wait. I want you to try on the uniform."

She went to the closet and took out the green, one-piece overall worn by workers in the New York Department of Sanitation. "He was as tall as you, but without your shoulders. It was loose on him. We can get another tomorrow if this one is too bad."

Shayne undressed and put on the uniform. It was too tight across the chest. The bulge of his .45 showed clearly. She gave him a critical looking over.

"Leave one more button open. No, I think you must carry the pistol in a bag."

Shayne grinned. "Between two slices of bread?"

"It will only be for a moment. Darling, that was clever of you, not to shoot for Ziggy. It pleased him. I have seen you with a pistol. I do not need to be shown."

"That's the way people get in the Marines—gun-happy."

"He is not so bad, after all," she said, trying to talk herself into it. "Perhaps tomorrow you must frighten him a little. He was frightened of Tug. Today they are all on edge about Tug's arrest, they drank too much. But what each one has to do is very simple indeed. There will be no trouble. We will arrive in Portugal, you and I, with no one the wiser and much money in our luggage."

"Maybe, Michele," Shayne said, his tone suddenly weary. "You don't know how it is, kid. It's never simple. There's always a place where you've got to hang tough or let them take you. Too goddamn many thieves really want to make mistakes so they'll be put away in a nice safe cell with three sure meals a day. This Tug character who let himself get picked up—after a couple of days with these oddballs maybe he was looking for a way out. He took the small pinch instead of the big one. And that's what these characters are thinking. They think he knew something."

"Stop it."

"It could work," he said. "So long as you remember it's going to take luck. And I have a feeling that the minute that cop recognized me in the subway, my luck changed. I may jinx this for you."

"Nonsense!" she said sharply. "We go over it and over it, if necessary a hundred times, and cut down the possibilities. Then if something unlucky happens, you will move quickly and decisively and overcome it. That is *my* feeling."

"I hope you're right."

She peered up at him. "Darling, that one policeman recognized you. What if there should be others? I believe we should at least dye your hair. Red, perhaps."

Startled, Shayne let out a snort of laughter. "And maybe we can talk Ziggy into loaning me his mustache. No, baby. If something happens, it happens. That's my philosophy." He picked up his jacket, which he had thrown on the bed, and felt in the side pocket. "I want to give you back your watch and bracelet."

CHAPTER 7

After she said goodnight, Shayne stripped off the Sanitation Department uniform and listened at the closed door. There was no lock but he manhandled the empty bureau in front of it. He went to the window. A room on the ground floor would have been better for his purposes, but there had been no way he could ask for one. He removed the sliding screen and swung out onto the shingled roof of the veranda, which ran around two sides of the house.

The shingles were dry and brittle underfoot. He edged carefully along the wall. The next window was lighted. He dropped to his knees and elbows and wriggled past. The shingles at the edge of the roof had split and peeled. The two-by-six beneath had begun to rot away from the nails. Shayne leaned on it and felt it give.

He heard a mumble of voices from the living room: Michele's and Szigetti's. The note of complaint in Szigetti's voice carried it around the house without bringing any words along with it. While the detective hesitated he noticed a dead branch dangling from the gutter. He might be able to use that.

He freed the branch carefully, then let it down heavy end first and worked the tip inside the copper wire leading to the telephone box. One of the thumbtacks pulled out of the clapboard. Rotating the branch, he caught the wire on a protruding twig and fished it up. Another tack popped out. In a moment, reaching down, he was able to seize the wire and pull it free.

There wasn't enough slack to reach his window. He unwound more wire from the outside of his battery case and performed a rough splice in the half-dark without tools. A rotten board gave way under his knee and he had to twist sideward to keep from going through.

Somebody had been moving in the bedroom on the other side of the wall. There was an abrupt silence. Shayne froze, spread-eagled on the roof.

Irene's voice said clearly, "You're beginning to jump, my girl."

She came to the lighted window to look out at the night. Shayne was too close to the wall to see her, but the shadow she cast was naked.

"Anybody out there?" she said in a low whisper. "If so, come in. No? Too bad, Irene. Another night shot to hell."

Shayne waited till her light was out. Springs jangled as she climbed into bed, and under cover of the noise he wriggled past. He climbed through his own window and replaced the screen.

On his bed, he doubled his pillow to make a soundproof cave for his tiny phone. He signaled the operator and gave her a number. An instant later the voice of his friend Tim Rourke spoke from the button in his ear.

"Mike?"

"Yeah," the detective said curtly into his cupped hands. "Tomorrow morning. Watch the ferry and the bridges. Dark green convertible." He gave the license number. "Read it back."

Rourke repeated the number. "Anything else?"

"No."

Rourke said, "Well, Mike, you did it. Sometimes you amaze me. Good luck, buddy."

Shayne withdrew the point of his screwdriver, breaking the connection. He moved the bureau away from the door. After sliding in under the sheet he put the hearing-aid button back in his ear. He smoked a last cigarette thoughtfully.

Like his friend Rourke, he was surprised at how well everything had gone. As Jake Melnick, the diamond dealer, Rourke had overdone the alarm and dismay, Shayne had thought, and when he had slapped the plastic membrane against his forehead he had produced a huge gush of blood, far more than would have been showing if Shayne had actually slugged him with a pistol. But the girl had been properly scared by it. Inspector Power himself had been the off-duty detective who accosted them in the lobby. The other roles had been filled by detectives from the Confidential Squad—the traffic patrolman outside, the workmen who blocked their escape with the piano, the uniformed cop, checking Michele's apartment, who had been hit in the face with a wet towel. Shayne smiled in the darknes. Only the plump lady in the flowered hat had not been part of the troupe, and her performance couldn't have been improved by three weeks of rehearsals. The one thing that had bothered Shayne—it hadn't seemed to bother Rourke or Power, he noticed—was whether he could convince an intelligent girl that he was capable of stunning a defenseless man with a .45, and then of putting a second bullet into a wounded cop. He made a wry face and stubbed out his cigarette. Perhaps the dyed hair made the difference.

The next day would be a difficult one. The day after that would be more difficult still. His main problem remained Michele, but he had no shortage of lesser problems. All Szigetti's early suspicions had come back, during the poker game, and Shayne's last look of the evening from the dapper former Marine had been hard and searching. Probably, Shayne thought, on one of Szigetti's vacation trips to Miami or Miami Beach some local companion had pointed Shayne out, and he could make the connection at any time. It was going to be like sitting in the same room with a ticking bomb.

There was a rapid series of clicks in his ear. He sat up, instantly alert, and adjusted the hearing-aid button.

"Yes?" a man's voice said.

"I found somebody," Michele's voice said without preamble.

"Excellent."

The half-swallowed consonants went with an upper-class English upbringing, Shayne thought, listening carefully, but there was also something else, a faint whiff of another country.

"I have observed him in action," Michele said, "and I think he will do well. After Wynanski I thought perhaps we should cancel everything and return to France. This one prides himself on common sense and directness and vulgarity, but there is something else too. I think he conducts himself as he imagines he should. He is flexible, he improvises well, and he unquestionably has courage. He can drink a great deal with little change in his manner. He lost his temper once or twice, but I think deliberately."

"I see you've been watching him closely," the voice said with a laugh.

"Yes, it was necessary that I do so. I have had to be careful with him. I will tell you about it later. I was in danger for a time. America! Never again, thank you. But I found that the danger stimulated the sexual responses to a surprising extent. Interesting. But I would dislike to have it happen again in just that way."

"Ah."

"Yes. He is desirable, this man, and I am wondering if I should take him to Europe with me. Perhaps not. But meanwhile, to be sure of him, I need a passport."

"That can be arranged."

"I have never met this precise type, you see, and at times I think he is not so simple. So you should know this. He shot a policeman during a robbery. His name is Francis McQuade. He is also wanted for a robbery in Brooklyn. Are you taking this down?"

"Yes."

"And all this gives us a lever. He must do as we say, to leave the country under our auspices."

There was a doubtful quality about the silence at the other end of the line. She said, "Don't you agree?"

"It could have that effect," the man said. "Or it could impair his judgment. There is a time to be reckless, a time to be prudent."

"Have confidence. If shooting becomes necessary, I want someone who will not hesitate. No shooting at all would be better, I quite agree. I have undertaken to pay him twenty-five thousand."

"Dollars, not francs, I suppose," the man said without enthusiasm. "This is becoming expensive. I don't say that in the way of criticism. The passport should be ready tomorrow at ten."

"Do you notice a noise on the line?"

"Nothing unusual. Except for those in the USSR, American phones are the noisiest in the world. Till tomorrow."

They hung up. Shayne chuckled to himself. His deal with the girl was for fifteen thousand, not twenty-five. Apparently her moneymaking instincts were as well developed as her sexual ones.

He disconnected the battery case. At the window he tugged at the wire until it pulled out of the telephone box below. He rewound it carefully. In a matter of minutes he was asleep.

Michele awakened him. He blinked up at her, wondering what he had done to deserve the attentions of this cool, elegant girl. Remembering where he was and what was expected of him, he reached out for her. She moved away quickly.

"Not now, darling. Not here. Those bedsprings would wake up everybody within miles."

"What's the matter with the floor?" Shayne suggested.

Her nose wrinkled. "I doubt that it has been cleaned since 1910. Put on some clothes and I'll see about breakfast."

She was wearing a straight up-and-down white linen dress, put together in a way that called the viewer's attention to the fact that Michele, inside it, was not straight up-and-down at all. It was no effort for Shayne to look at her with admiring lust.

"I mean it," she said. "I have an appointment at ten. Meanwhile, we have much to prepare. But sometime today, I promise you! In the bathroom at the end of the corridor you will find shaving things."

Shayne shaved and dressed. As he left the bedroom he had a feeling that his preparations were incomplete, and he went back for the dummy hearing aid. In the kitchen he found Michele preparing an omelet. She made a face from the stove.

"Orange juice from a can. Coffee in the form of powder. Margarine. How do people live this way?"

"We get used to it."

"Darling, after this is finished I cook for you. Cooking is an art all French girls are required to know."

The omelet was light and excellent, and Shayne had it to himself, Michele contenting herself with a half cup of coffee and a bite of roll. Brownie appeared as they were leaving. He regarded them with sad, bloodshot eyes.

"I can't find the aspirin," he said accusingly.

"Billy will drive down and get you some," Michele said. "Tell everyone else to stay inside, and please not to drink so much. It will be nice if no one has a headache tomorrow."

Brownie mumbled something and watched them go.

Shayne said, "I'd better drive. That's the way we do it in this country."

In the car, heading down the long bumpy driveway, he went on, "To get something off my chest right away—this Szigetti is supposed to cover me, the way I understand it. I don't trust the guy. I know it's too late to work in anybody else, but I want him over on the other side of the truck so I can keep an eye on him. If he quits on me, I want to know it."

"Yes-s," she said doubtfully. "See what you think when we get there."

Shayne drove through the electric eye at the gate and turned left. New houses were going up everywhere. At the first crossroads, there were a few stores, a bar and grill, a gas station.

"Left again," she said.

"I want a paper."

"We're in a hurry, darling. Get one in the city."

"I want to see what kind of story they gave me."

He swung onto the asphalt apron in front of the grocery store. There was a rack of New York newspapers on the front step.

"Give me a *News*," he called.

A woman tending the stand whipped a *Daily News* out of her stack and brought it to him. He tossed it in Michele's lap and drove on.

A jet had crashed near Kennedy Airport, killing 83, so Shayne's small-scale act of violence hadn't been given a page-one headline. Michele found the story on page three and read it in silence. Shayne, of course, already knew what it said. Rourke had written the story and Power had persuaded the editor of the *News* to plant it in one copy of one edition, in return for a promise of an inside track on later developments. And then the single doctored copy had been planted on the Staten Island rack and the woman had been told to sell it to no one but a big black-haired man driving a green Chevrolet convertible.

"But he wasn't a policeman at all!" Michele exclaimed.

"What?"

"For twenty years he was a policeman, then he had to resign because of a gambling scandal. Edward Farrell, fifty-six. The last two years, he has been wandering about the city hoping to see some criminal to arrest, so the police would take him back. It is a de Maupassant story!"

"My heart bleeds," Shayne said. "What's it say about Melnick?"

"In a coma still."

"He better *stay* in a coma."

"Condition critical," she said, reading. "That means serious? Perhaps by the time he comes round you and I will be in a country where few people can speak English."

"Knock on wood," Shayne said.

On the plane between Miami and New York, he had studied New York and Long Island road maps, and he knew that there were four possible ways for a car to get off Staten Island. When Michele gave him another left, in the direction of Port Richmond, he knew they were going by ferry. Victory Boulevard took them into St. George. This was a bad time of the day for automobiles. They inched down to the ferry slip. After a ten-minute wait they were permitted to crawl aboard a Manhattan ferry. They stayed in the car, and Shayne read the *Daily News* story.

"The things they always get wrong," he said, and paged through the paper until he came to Dick Tracy, the world's most preposterous sleuth. He snorted again a moment later, wadded the paper up and threw it in a trash basket as they arrived at the Battery.

From here he was expected to know the way by himself. Concentrating hard, he pulled an imaginary map into focus, with its tiny street designations and little blue arrows.

"What do we want, the West Side Highway?"

"I think so. The quickest way to Sixth Avenue and Twenty-seventh."

Most of the traffic was moving north on Whitehall Street, and Shayne moved with it. In addition to street signs and traffic signals, he watched for illegally parked cars. He saw what he was looking for, an unmarked black Ford at a bus stop, where it could swing left on Whitehall or take the East Side elevated highway. Two men were in the front seat, and one of them was Jake Melnick, no longer in a coma, the blood washed off his face, and changed back into Shayne's friend Tim Rourke.

Shayne slowed and changed lanes, letting the Ford get in behind him. He turned off at Bowling Green, swinging the wheel with a show of confidence he was far from feeling. Several blocks later, he stumbled on an inconspicuous ramp leading upward to the West Side Highway. He left at Twenty-third Street, the black Ford still right behind him. He passed Eighth Avenue, then Seventh, and came to the Avenue of the Americas. Here a red light stopped him.

"Our Sanitation truck," Michele said, looking down the avenue, "will come all the way uptown on Sixth. We have timed the distance, five days in a row. To be safe we should leave a thirty-minute margin."

Now Shayne remembered that the Avenue of the Americas was the official name for Sixth, and he turned north when the light changed.

"You're sure of the route?" he said.

"Very sure."

As they approached Twenty-seventh Street she said, "Now stop a bit."

Shayne double-parked short of the corner. There was a solid line of parked cars in the metered spaces against the curb, and the second line was also nearly solid.

"Billy is to fix the light this afternoon," Michele said. "Brownie and Irene will come from there. Ziggy from there."

She pointed, and explained what would happen when the truck halted at the corner. It wasn't simple, but it was less complex than the average football play on the college level. Shayne's only reservation was that the play would be executed by a pickup team of misfits and malcontents.

"Now if you want Ziggy to do anything different—" she said.

"No," Shayne said slowly. "I won't make my move before he commits himself. It looks good, kid. Somebody put a lot of brain work into this."

"Thank you," she said with a blinding smile.

"How long does the light stay red?"

"Forever, until a repairman finds the button. Billy's plan is to attach it to the back of the one-way arrow. It will be hard to find. Are we finished here?"

Shayne looked over the terrain once again. As soon as the Sanitation truck began to move, the group on the sidewalk would fade into nearby buildings. In back, there was a low wall to climb. Two parked cars would be waiting on Twenty-sixth Street. They had worked out two alternate routes in case anything happened to this one.

"Now," she said, "what you are to do, darling, you go through the red light and turn right."

"You mean left."

"No, right, against the arrow. What will happen, the moment the light changes here when Billy pushes the button, a truck will back out halfway to Broadway, to block both lanes. All the cars between there and here will drain off on the green light. There will be nothing in your way. Take me around and I show you."

He went on to Twenty-eighth, where he made a legal

right turn and turned right again on Broadway. On Twenty-seventh he went west, toward Sixth.

"Here," she said. She pointed into a sloping delivery alley between two loft buildings. "Leave the car and walk in and see."

He went into a paved yard behind the buildings. A wall of steel posts and panels barred the way at the property line.

He returned to the girl. "It's blind. A hell of a place to unload."

"We do not unload here, my love. You are concerned about the wall? Simply put the truck in low, point at the wall and keep going. The uprights have been cut. They are held in place now by aluminum brackets. A child's perambulator could knock it over. No, not a perambulator, but a large and powerful garbage truck, certainly. There is another alley exactly beyond. Drive through to Twenty-eighth, turn right with the traffic. Thus we confuse everybody."

Shayne was grinning broadly. "Baby, you're in the wrong line of work. You should be a lady professor. What if another truck is already down in there?"

"The lofts in this building are all vacant," she said. "It is soon to be taken down. And we have two wooden barriers. 'Police Department, No Passing.' We put one here, one on Twenty-eighth. They are of flimsy wood. You knock them over and drive on. More questions?"

"No more questions," he said, still grinning. "Honey, I think we're going to take these people!"

"Of course we are," she said simply. "Now I show you where we truly unload."

Shayne circled the block again and headed down Broadway, shifting to Fifth where Broadway crossed it at Madison Square. She pointed out an excavation for a new building on Twenty-first, between Fifth and Sixth. A wooden wall had been thrown up along the sidewalk. The site could be entered by a sloping dirt roadway.

"We borrow this place," she said. "No one will be working. Change clothes while they unload. Then leave the truck on another block. Take a taxi to LaGuardia Airport. There I am waiting." She looked at her watch. "Now I am late, dear. Go uptown to Forty-second Street."

Shayne turned again on Sixth. In a moment more they passed the corner of Twenty-seventh, where, if everything went well, there would be a certain amount of activity the next day.

"One thing you haven't covered," Shayne said. "How about the two men in the cab, where do we dump them?"

"Billy will carry four sets of handcuffs. As soon as you are out of sight behind the building between Twenty-seven and Twenty-eight, put handcuffs on their wrists and ankles, and leave them."

Shayne shook his head. "Kid, why aren't you a millionaire?"

"I intend to be," she said.

At Forty-second Street she told him to turn west. During all the weaving and circling, the black Ford had clung to their tail. It made the turn behind them.

"You need a picture for the passport," she said. "I think I remember a sign—yes, there."

She pointed to an arcade filled with low-cost entertainment devices, including a photo booth. She waited while Shayne ducked inside, coming back a moment later with a strip of four shots of a glowering, unprepossessing face which bore very little resemblance to his real one.

"Frightful," she said. "But never mind. Now I must be apart from you briefly, darling. It is to collect some money, so be patient. I will leave you at a cinema, and come as soon as I can. I hope in an hour's time."

She scanned the marquees of the double-feature houses they were passing. "These are all dreadful! Well." She pointed to a theatre showing two of the dubbed Italian spectacles which Shayne was always careful to avoid. "That one. I need some money. Give me some please."

Shayne counted out five twenties and gave them to her. He kissed her cheek and got out. She moved over behind the wheel, sliding the seat forward.

"If there's no smoking downstairs I'll be in the mezzanine," he said.

Crossing the street, he bought a ticket at the glassed-in booth. Michele's Chevy still hadn't moved. He waved at her and went in.

CHAPTER 8

Shayne strode purposefully past the candy counter, apparently anxious not to miss a minute of the movie, which dealt with the adventures of Jason among the Amazons, female warriors who were almost as bare-chested as Jason himself. The theatre was half-filled. The customers were almost all men, most of them sitting alone, many of them asleep. Shayne ignored the usher, went down an outside aisle toward a red Exit sign, and pushed through a heavy door leading into a narrow cul de sac separating this theatre from the next. By the time he reached the sidewalk the Chevy and the police Ford had both disappeared.

He shut himself in a phone booth in the amusement arcade. The number where he could reach Rourke during the day was scrawled across the back of one of the cards in his wallet. He dialed the Manhattan mobile operator and read her the number. Rourke answered promptly.

"Shayne. Where are you, Tim?"

"Going into the bus terminal," Rourke told him. "She's right ahead. There's a garage on the roof. How come she dropped you?"

"She has a ten-o'clock date with the guy we're after. She said she'd be back in an hour. How about the cop they gave you, does he seem OK?"

"So far, but how can you tell? When she parks, you want him to follow her?"

"Right. He has to be the one to do it. You're supposed to be in the hospital with a fractured skull. Tell him not to lose her. This is our best chance, maybe our only one."

"There she goes!" Rourke said. "Hold on."

Shayne heard the roar of buses and other automobile noises from the other end of the connection. Rourke spoke in a low voice to the driver of the Ford. The toll operator cut in to tell Shayne she needed more money, and he put in another coin.

Rourke said, "It's underway. She's waiting for the elevator and Jamieson's right behind her. He'll call back on this phone as soon as he puts her in anywhere. I'm in touch with Power."

"Let's not tie up the phone, then," Shayne said. "How far away are you?"

"Next block. A big hunk of concrete. You'll see it."

Shayne decided to stay in the arcade another few minutes, to give Michele time to get out of the neighborhood. He paid a dime to send five rubber balls tumbling into a maze of baffles and holes. As each ball dropped, a playing card lit up on the backboard. It turned out that Shayne had rolled a full house and won a stuffed panda, to his disgust. He gave it to a Puerto Rican girl who was watching the play, and returned to the street.

At the big Port Authority bus terminal on Eighth Avenue and Forty-first Street, an elevator took him to the parking garage on the top floor. Rourke, standing beside the Ford, saw him and waved.

The reporter grinned happily as he approached. "That hair, Mike. You could walk down Biscayne Boulevard and nobody'd know you."

"How's your skull?"

"The skull's fine," Rourke said. "It's my belly that's sore. You were supposed to pull that punch."

"I wanted you to make a convincing noise. I thought you did it very well."

"That wasn't acting," Rourke said sourly. "All I've got to say, it's lucky I'm in top shape physically."

Shayne exchanged an amused look with his friend, who had taken no exercise for years and who lived almost entirely on cigarettes, bad whiskey and delicatessen sandwiches. Some day he would probably fall apart. Meanwhile he wasn't letting it bother him.

Shayne folded his big frame into the front seat of the Ford. Rourke came in beside him.

"That babe is really something," Rourke observed. "I suppose you're making out all right?"

"Within reason," Shayne said shortly.

"She surprised me, you know? She's got too much class for this job, like a stakes winner in a claiming race. What makes a doll like that tick? I'll never know."

"She wants to make a million bucks," Shayne said. "Don't ask me why. Where's Power?"

"Downtown. He's keeping a phone free. I don't suppose you read the morning paper?"

"All about the sudden death of an ex-cop? Yeah, I read it on the ferry. There were a couple of Tim Rourke touches there I liked."

"That's not what I mean." He reached into the back seat for a *Daily News,* which was folded open to an inside page. "And this one ran in all copies of all editions."

Frowning, Shayne took the paper. It was a small item, alone on a page with a department-store ad and headlined, SPURNED COP SLAYS SELF. Sergeant Herman Kraus, 33, the police department's chief property clerk, had been found in his Bronx apartment, his service revolver beside his bed, a bullet in his brain. He had been in the department nine years, a sergeant for three. He had served two years in the Army. He was survived by a married sister in Ashtabula, Ohio. Friends said that Kraus, a bachelor, had been despondent since becoming estranged from his fiancée. They had quarreled over her friendships with other men.

Shayne let out his breath in a soundless whistle.

"Yeah," Rourke said. "Quite a coincidence. He's the guy who handled the bookkeeping on the narcotics evidence. When an envelope went to court, he signed it out. When it came back, he signed it in. He had charge of the whole operation tomorrow. The key man, in short. This all comes from Power. One important thing he didn't tell me. Apparently there's a suicide note. I'm a friend of yours, so I must be reasonably kosher, but I'm also a newspaperman, and he's keeping that in mind. But it happens I know a rewrite man on the *News*, I've known him for years. He told me about the note."

"What's in it?"

"Mike, you know the way the cops are when another cop knocks himself off. It's usually not because of sweetheart trouble, and the lid goes on. They call in the department heads, and decide how much has to come out. Preferably nothing. Then they let it out with an eyedropper, one drop at a time. They're saving that note till they see how it goes."

Shayne read the uninformative little story again. "Nobody in his right mind would try anything like this tomorrow without an inside man. And my Michele is definitely in her right mind. Quite a coincidence is right."

"That's the impression I get," Rourke said. "Maybe Kraus sold it to her, and then got cold feet at the last minute. Maybe somebody else found out about it and gave him the gentleman's choice—suicide or a public jam."

"Power can't hope to sit on it forever."

"No, but through tomorrow? The way I get it, and you never did start with A and go right through to Z, he wants the stickup to go off without a hitch. The wrong kind of newspaper story would kill it. It's bad enough as it stands. If your babe has really been doing business with Kraus, she's going to stop and do some hard thinking. What if he blew the whole thing to somebody before he pulled the trigger?"

Shayne considered. "Did it make all the papers?"

"Not the *Times* or the *Trib*. It'll be in the afternoons. Oh. I see what you're getting at. She didn't see the *News*. If you can keep her occupied, so she doesn't look at the papers—yeah. Now how will you manage that, I wonder?"

"Maybe I can think of something."

Rourke grinned. "Is it too late to change places? You be Melnick, the diamond man. I'll be McQuade."

The phone rang. The reporter was wound up tight; he leaped at it and got it before the ring was complete.

"Rourke." He listened for only a moment. "Tell it to Shayne. He's right here."

He passed the phone to Shayne. "Go ahead," the detective said.

"Jamieson. I've lost her, and what am I supposed to do now?"

Shayne felt a sudden pounding behind his eyes. "What do you mean, you've lost her?"

"She's in a building, and I can only cover one exit at a time."

Shayne swore under his breath. "Where are you?"

"Downtown. We came down on the Eighth Avenue. She went in a bank on William Street, across from the Chase Manhattan. Geneva Credit and Deposit. That was at ten-twenty. It's a funny bank, Shayne—you go in and there's a kind of living room, with easy chairs and a fireplace yet. This senior citizen sitting at a desk with black cuffs. No sign of the woman. I told him I was looking for a place to cash a check and pulled the hell out."

"How many exits?"

"One other I can't see. But there are tunnels everywhere in this part of town. If she wants to leave me sitting here, God knows she can do it. She did some hanging around looking in windows before she went in. Whether she spotted me or not, I couldn't tell you." He added abruptly, "Here she comes."

The phone clattered in Shayne's ear. He looked at his watch.

"Get anything?" Rourke asked.

"An address. What's Power's number?"

Rourke told him. "That's a direct line. He doesn't want any news from you or me coming in through the switchboard."

Shayne gave the mobile operator the number. In a moment Power's crisp, controlled voice said hello.

"Mike!" he exclaimed when he heard Shayne's voice. "Wait a minute, I want to close the door."

A moment later he was back on the line. "It's getting so I don't even trust myself. Everything under control?"

"Everything's fine," Shayne told him. "We've got a tentative address for the banker. Jamieson can give you the details. About Kraus."

"Oh, you saw that? Did she see it?"

"Not yet."

"I don't know how you're situated, Mike, but if there's any chance of keeping her in the dark, for God's sake do it. The name shouldn't mean anything to anyone else. So far it's not much of a story. The trouble is, he left a confession. I'm doing my damnedest to keep it from the press, and so far I've succeeded."

"Does he mention Michele?"

"Luckily, no. But we know he was feeding her information, because we've seen them together. The proverbial bad apple. He's been living well over his income, and the note explains where he's been getting the money. Do you have time for this, Mike?"

"A couple of minutes. Go ahead."

"He's been stealing drugs from the case files. Steamed open the envelopes and substituted cornstarch for heroin. I doubt if it amounted to much in terms of volume, but once he took that first step they could put on the pressure and he had to go along. Last night he apparently decided he couldn't go through with it. The note doesn't mention the robbery. He must have thought his suicide by itself would take care of that, we'd have to cancel the shipment to check through to find out how far the substitutions went."

Shayne said, "Is there any chance that it wasn't suicide?"

"A chance," Power said doubtfully. "He wouldn't be the first informer to end up with a hole in the head instead of ten percent of the loot. It's an idea, Mike, but we'll have to put it aside for the time being. Is there anything I ought to know about tomorrow?"

"No, except that it looks damned good. As far as I can see, she's thought of everything."

"I hope not *everything*," Power said.

He wished Shayne luck and the detective put back the phone.

"Mike, to finish up about Kraus," Rourke said. "I talked to the Bronx legman who phoned in that story and I picked up a few points. The girl's name, for one thing."

"You mean the fiancée?"

"That's too big a word. They were going together, that's all. They had a date last night. I thought I might go up and talk to her, but I really meant it when I said we ought to change places. Getting the feel of this kind of situation isn't one of the things I do best. Hell, I'll do what I can."

Shayne thought about it, his hand on the door latch. "I might be able to get out tonight, late. Could you bring her over to Staten Island? There's an intersection down the road from the house. A tavern, a couple of stores. Don't be surprised if I don't show up. It depends on how it goes."

He gave Rourke directions, and Rourke promised to try to have the girl there around midnight.

"Hey, I almost forgot. I brought you a jug."

He took a pint of Courvoisier out of his coat pocket and handed it to Shayne. The detective opened it and took a long drink.

"That's sweet liquor," he said, handing it back regretfully. "Keep it for me. I'm disguised as a blended-whiskey drinker."

CHAPTER 9

The bored blonde in the ticket cage did a double take as Shayne bought a second admission. Even with dyed hair he carried an atmosphere that made him easy to remember. An unlighted cigarette in his mouth, he went up to the mezzanine. There were several pairs of young lovers there, a flock of alert, chattering homosexuals, several sleeping derelicts, a small handful of people actually watching the screen.

Shayne took a seat in a half-empty row, and soon closed his eyes. Presently a would-be pickpocket slid into the seat next to him. Shayne opened his eyes.

"Get far away from me, kid."

The boy bridled. "Did—did you sign a lease on this seat?" he demanded, stuttering.

Shayne looked at him in the flickering light and the boy scurried away. Ten minutes later Michele took his place. Shayne's eyes were closed again, but he could smell her perfume amid the reek of tobacco and other odors.

"How's the picture?" she said.

"How's the picture," he said in disgust, sitting up and stretching. "Let's get out of here."

"With pleasure."

She had brought a thin cowhide dispatch case. She resisted for an instant when he took it from her.

"Ladies don't carry luggage when there's a man along," he said.

One of the homosexuals cut a slanting look at him as they passed up the aisle. "Isn't he *masculine?*" he remarked to a friend.

Outside the theatre, Shayne said, "I want to buy a couple of shirts. Why don't we decide where we're going, and I'll meet you?"

She took his arm. "Darling, you are sometimes funny. I would hate to mislay you at this stage. With the money in that case, plus a passport, you could disappear to Brazil and grow a big beard to go with a new name."

"Why didn't I think of that?" Shayne said.

"Because you know I would not allow it," she told him. "You need more than shirts. I like to go shopping with a man, but I warn you. I have definite opinions."

She signaled an eastbound taxi. "Brooks Brothers," she told the driver.

When Shayne protested she said sweetly, "It is expensive there, but you have money to spend. This I can say of my own knowledge. And what would you spend it on otherwise?"

"Girls. Booze. Hell, I don't know. I never have any trouble spending money."

"Spend some of it on clothes, to please me, darling."

Shayne looked at his unpressed garbardine. "What's the matter with this suit?"

"What was the matter with the movie?"

The taxi took them up Madison Avenue and Michele marched Shayne into the citadel of correct gentlemen's apparel. He submitted meekly, to the extent of six shirts, ties and a pair of Peale shoes on the main floor. The second floor yielded two suits, and the third, a sports jacket and slacks. Shayne balked at walking shorts, but gave in on a Locke hat. On the top floor, Michele exerted her full charm and exacted a promise that cuffs would be put on the pants by the end of the afternoon. Shayne paid cash all the way, and on the down-ride bought an English suitcase to put everything in.

Another taxi took them back to the Port Authority garage, where they transferred to Michele's Chevy. She was bubbling with excitement.

"And now, darling!"

"Now we buy a bottle and some sandwiches and go to bed."

"Yes! Hurry."

He drove uptown on Eighth Avenue, stopping first at a delicatessen, then at a liquor store. In the liquor store he bypassed the shelves loaded with cognacs, and picked out a fifth of mediocre bourbon. Farther up Eighth, he turned into one of the big motels.

"Darling?" Michele said. "I thought my apartment. I might have a phone call."

The same thought had occurred to Shayne. She couldn't be told about the death of Herman Kraus if nobody knew where she was.

"I'm thinking about that dame in the hat," he said. "Remember? She had a good long look at me, and I'm still wearing the same suit. I don't want it to happen again. This time she might not faint."

"Oh, *merde*, you are right, of course."

He registered as Mr. and Mrs. Matt Maguire, of Rochester, New York. They were given a room on the eighth floor. It was a motel room, with no particular pluses or minuses. As she passed the TV she automatically switched it on. A solemn man was reading news bulletins. Shayne turned it off.

"Who wants to look at that crap?"

He pulled off his tie and jacket and made the drinks. Then he opened the dispatch case.

"Seven thousand, five hundred," she said, watching him, "minus seven hundred and three."

"What seven hundred and three?"

"You took eight hundred and three from me last night, and gave me back a hundred."

Shayne grinned and dumped the packages of bills on the bureau. "Just for the hell of it, I think I'll count it. Anybody can make a mistake, and the thing about you, baby, if there's a mistake I know it'll be in your favor."

"You'll find it all there," she said coolly.

He counted it carefully, verifying that count with a second one. His expression became more and more thoughtful.

"Where'd you take your commission, off the top?"

"My commission? The word hardly applies, does it? The terms were clear. You agreed to them."

He shook out a cigarette. It was the last in the package, and he wadded the package angrily and threw it across the room.

"Whose capital are you using? What the hell are you trying to pull off tomorrow? I don't like this keep-him-in-the-dark business. You've got the moves all worked out. What I'm starting to wonder, are there a couple of moves at the end you didn't tell me about?"

"What is your complaint, exactly?" she said with no change of expression.

"There are too many twists in this thing! I don't want to end up in some waiting room at LaGuardia with egg on my face. The payoff, the payoff. Where do I draw the rest of the fifteen thousand?"

She said coolly, "If you wish, you can pick it up when you deliver the truck. I can have it there in cash, waiting. The passport is in order. I have arranged for us to leave together, but if you prefer to stay in New York and take your chances, I think in a moment or two I could manage to forget you."

"That I believe," Shayne said, blowing out smoke.

"But what brought this on? I have done as I promised. Perhaps you think it is easy to produce an American passport on twelve hours' notice. It is far from easy. What has come over you all at once?"

"It hit me," Shayne said, biting it off. "This is new country for me, kid. I went on one other joint job once, just once. Two other guys, and if you went by what they said they were very hard boys. It was a nice score, a hundred and twenty for the three of us. Then my wheelman got picked up on a murder rap, and on that they really had him. Before the D.A. let him cop a second-degree plea, he had to tell them every last thing he ever did, including *my* name and address. And the second guy wasn't satisfied with forty G's. He decided to go for eighty, only I jumped just in time. Two inches of the knife blade broke off between my ribs—I can show you the scar. By the time I finished with him I think he was sorry. *I* ended up with eighty. What I mean is—I made myself a promise. It had to be something I could do myself from then on, or forget it. Don't worry, I'm not copping out," he said when she started to speak. "But hell, from your own point of view, you'll get better service if I know more about it."

He gestured at the window. "That isn't a chessboard out there. It's a city full of cars and people. You tell me to turn left at such and such a corner. What if somebody's digging a hole in the street and I can't turn left? You've got to leave some of it up to me. And if I don't know any more tomorrow than I do now, I can guarantee you I'll make the wrong move."

"To be specific," she said.

"A garbage truck, for God's sake! With two cops on the tailgate! OK, is it the kind of garbage you want me to dump in the sewer if I get in trouble? If I can't get in touch with you, who do I get in touch with? What kind of protection have we got?"

She put down her drink. Coming over to his chair in her stocking feet, she kissed the corner of his mouth. "You are making a large Alp out of a small bump in the ground, you know. Number one: we have no protection. Let us be careful not to be caught. Number two: I can't see what difference it makes, but if you must know what will be in the truck—"

She began unbuttoning his shirt. "It will begin its journey at a police warehouse, and end at an incinerator. The police in New York have collected certain evidence against some important people, and these people, I must tell you, do have connections. They are the existing organization in certain illegal areas."

"Are you talking about the Mafia or something?"

"Oh, the Mafia. It is true that many of them are Sicilians, South Italians of the second generation in America, but it is not the kind of group you think of when you say Mafia. This evidence, some is serious, some is merely business information. By pulling strings, by spending money, they have persuaded the police to burn it, and *my* friends, who would like a share in the profitable affairs controlled by the Mafia, wish to seize it before it can reach the incinerator."

"Why? I must be dumber than I thought. I don't get it."

"Darling, one doesn't ask why. The Mafia people are vulnerable, you know. The times have passed them by. In the days of jet travel, they think and do business in the old slow way. My friends will say to them in effect, 'Here are Xerox copies of certain documents in our possession. Retire.' Now. To answer another question. If you find yourself unable to reach the transfer point, do not empty the truck in the sewer. Call me at a number I will give you."

Shayne uttered a coarse expletive. "I'm over my head here, baby. It's not my kind of deal. The sooner I get back in my own league, the better for everybody."

"You set your sights too low, darling," she said, smiling. "Wait till you see yourself in your new clothes."

Shayne's voice had begun to lose its edge. "I've had chicks try to change me before. I forget their names."

"I don't want to change you. I want to change your surroundings. You have no objection to being rich, surely?"

"I've been in the chips once or twice," he said. "But a funny thing about stickup dough. It's not like real money."

"I get you real money," she said. "And the real money today, you are right, is honest money. That's what these Mafia primitives will never understand, with their codes, their quickness to commit murder for something of utterly no importance, like an insult."

"I don't know what the hell you're talking about," Shayne said. All the anger was gone from his voice.

"I tell you then." She left her perch, whirled around with her arms raised, and came back to the arm of the chair and kissed him hard. "You make me feel *excellent*. When I was a young girl there was no money in my family. Only a few lucky ones had work in that region, so my mother went away to the city. She was a handsome woman, men gave her money, she sent some to us in our village, so we ate not badly. But always she thought her manner of living sinful. Wrong, right, what did it matter, who decided it was right to sit in the house without a sou and go to political meetings and come home hungry? My father said it was society one should blame, the system of government, but I learned from my mother, not my father. He died of pneumonia, it was called. Some years later I was the friend of a rich man, who had tankers and passenger vessels and three yachts and much besides. He started from a hungry family like mine. He taught me about making money, it amused him. First, he said, you accumulate a small sum so you have something to risk. That one time it may be necessary to break a law or so, which is all right if you go in fast and get out fast. But after that you hire lawyers, who take excellent care that you no longer break laws. If it is necessary to be cruel, be cruel, but within the law. I listened carefully. And I have many ideas. I have come to know many useful people. I think I do well."

"Baby—" Shayne scowled, trying to put his thoughts into words without going outside the character he was pretending to be. He gave it up with a disgusted wave. "If that's your idea of living."

"It is very much my idea of living," she said. "I know women are not expected to become rich except when a rich husband dies of an early heart attack. It is all right for a man to be hard and ruthless, not a woman. I need a man to work with me, who is not a slave of sentimentality, who can move, who can do what is necessary."

Again Shayne let his voice take on a hard edge. "And who shot a cop in the States? I can see how you figure, baby. I'll have to jump when you crack the whip, or New York gets a long-distance phone call, the full details on where they can find me."

She said quietly, "I hope I can think of some way to show you that isn't so."

"I hope so too, baby, but that's all right. I'm a hard man to push. Right now you and I are going in the same direction. Maybe we'll make it as far as Portugal. But don't make any long-range plans. I've never been with a dame longer than two months."

"But two months! It is an age!" she said with a delighted smile. "Darling, I knew we would agree."

Shayne shook his head wryly. "One thing I *will* say. I never met anybody like you."

"Take off your gun."

"In a minute."

"No, at once. So you are a hard man to push?"

Her mouth came down to his and he felt her probing tongue. There was something he had to do, he remembered. He had to keep her from listening to the news or reading the afternoon papers.

Without opening her eyes, she whispered, "Unfasten your pistol."

"That's not pushing," he said. "That's pulling. I'm an easy man to pull. Unfasten it yourself."

"Where, here?"

He showed her. She showed him how to unfasten her white dress.

When Shayne noticed the time again, the afternoon was gone.

CHAPTER 10

They made it to Brooks Brothers as the store was closing, and picked up Shayne's slacks and the pants to his new suits. He made one other stop, outside Grand Central.

"I want to stash the dough and pick up some liquor," he said, reaching for the dispatch case. "Won't take a minute."

"You will be back?"

He gave her a direct look. "What do you think?"

He stopped at a liquor store in the arcade and bought two fifths of bourbon. He didn't have to look around to know that she had left the car on the street and followed him in. He went down to the men's room on the lower level. He paid a dime for a booth, opened the dispatch case and put in the diamonds he had taken from Tim Rourke the night before. They were real diamonds. He put the forged passport in his pocket.

He checked the dispatch case in a coin locker and started back to the street, giving Michele time to get there ahead of him. She smiled at him brightly as he got in.

"Please do not do that again, darling. It took longer than a minute, and bad things happened to my insides."

He leaned across and gravely kissed her cheek. "Stop worrying."

"I bought a paper while I waited. I thought you might—"

He snapped off the ignition. "Use your head. There's a trash basket over there—get rid of it."

She didn't like his tone, but after an instant's hesitation she took the folded *World-Journal* to the receptacle and dumped it.

Shayne's face was still angry when she came back. "What if one of those psychos out on Staten Island reads about the cop-shooting and gets the idea it might be me? We have enough on our hands."

"I am sorry."

"The hell with it."

He missed the Forty-first Street entrance to the Franklin D. Roosevelt Drive and had to come back for it, but that was something even native New Yorkers must occasionally do, he thought. The little flare-up had gone no further, and they rode in silence with the radio tuned to the only sound available on A.M. stations at this hour, the pounding music currently popular among American teen-agers.

"We have it in France as well," she told him. "If one could only understand the words."

Much against Shayne's will, he found himself beginning to like her, although he knew she was as phony as a three-dollar bill. Given a slight turn of circumstances, say a father with a job when she was growing up—

Unless, he thought suddenly, there had been no truth in that story about a poverty-stricken father and a roving mother? It could be, he told himself; it could very well be. There would always be a question with this girl where the truth stopped and the lying began.

Billy was watching for them inside the gate. "Better get up there very sudden," he told Michele. "Spaghetti's stoned. He's trying to get a rise out of Brownie, and I can tell you that cat ain't going to sit still much longer."

Shayne came down hard on the gas.

"This is impossible, it has to stop," she said.

"Yeah."

He skidded to a fast stop in the gravel. An instant later, striding into the living room, he found an unshaven, bleary-eyed Szigetti, in a dirty sleeveless undershirt, cleaning his revolver on the sofa. Brownie was sitting across the room reading a paperback sex novel. He seemed indifferent to Szigetti, but Shayne saw that he was sweating. Irene was putting polish on her nails and drinking red wine. She looked up at Shayne, her eyes bright.

"Welcome."

Michele clicked past Shayne. "Everything peaceful, the way I like it."

"Look at that book," Szigetti said thickly. "A bare-assed white girl on the cover. Inside just one juicy rape after another."

"Your choice of reading matter seems to be irritating Ziggy," Michele observed to Brownie. "Can you find something else? Has anybody eaten?"

Szigetti went on, "The only reason he picked it up was to see if he could get my ass. All he's doing is holding it. He can't be reading—I don't see him moving his lips."

"That will be enough!" Michele snapped.

Szigetti finished assembling his .38, spun the cylinder and took deliberate aim at Brownie.

"It's empty," he said with a mocking grin, "but will you look at the man sweat?"

Brownie looked up from the book. "Kid stuff."

Szigetti's upper lip lifted and he pulled the trigger. The hammer clicked down on nothing. He repeated his mocking laugh.

Shayne walked in front of the .38, towering over the drunken gunman.

"Out of the line of fire," Szigetti said mildly.

"There's one bullet in the gun," Irene warned. "I saw it."

Shayne bent down over Szigetti, who still held the .38 extended in firing position. The muzzle touched Shayne's chest.

"We need a drink," Shayne said. "I brought a couple of bottles back with me."

"Buddy. Please. One more. Six to one is good odds."

"Try it on me. But if you pull the trigger you'd better hope it hits the live round."

"Why should I do a dumb thing like that?" the smaller man protested. "Too few ex-Marines in the world as it is."

"Please!" Michele said. "Have a drink, stop this silliness."

Shayne, the .38 still touching his chest, took hold of Szigetti's arms and began applying pressure. He slowly backed away, bringing Szigetti to his feet after him.

"What are they feeding you, red wine?" Shayne said. "That stuff eats out the stomach lining. Let's have a couple of jolts of booze."

He continued to squeeze, and Szigetti's body began to twist. He stopped resisting suddenly and the .38 fell to the coffee table, knocking over a can of gun oil.

"You still keep in shape, don't you, Sarge?"

Shayne let him go. Picking up the revolver, he broke it and spun the cylinder. There were no rounds showing.

"He palmed it on you," he said to Irene. "Russian roulette without bullets. You can't lose."

"You got to do something to pass the time," Szigetti said. "Where's that bottle?"

Shayne brought in his suitcase and the liquor from the car. Irene came into the kitchen with him and leaned against him while he was getting the ice.

"Remember the last time I brought up the subject and you said later?" she said. "Like how much later?"

"Like I'm tied up, kid, if you know what I mean."

"Oh, I do," she said gloomily. "Michele, huh? I don't suppose she'd consider making it a threesome?"

"You never know," Shayne said, breaking ice out of the tray. "I'll ask."

"Well, I know you won't, when you say it like that. And I thought this was going to be so different. It's as much of a drag as anything else." She yawned. "Excuse me. I keep yawning, for some reason."

"A simple case of nervous stomach," he said. "Even the world's champion gets sick the night before a big fight. There's a lot riding on this tomorrow, baby, but it's going to click. It has that feel."

"I thought so at first, but now I don't know. Tug getting picked up and everything. All I had to do, Tug said, was get out there on the street and scream. He didn't say anything about hanging around for four days beforehand. He's my current guy, did anybody tell you? It's an open secret. It was OK when he was here. I wouldn't feel this way if I had a little nuzzling to look forward to. Now I suppose you think I'm a nympho."

"What's that?"

"You know as well as I do," she said with a smile. "Well, I'm not. I'm normal. It's stage fright! I get nightmares, I need somebody to hang onto. Brownie won't because he's sort of scared of Ziggy. Ziggy can't. He claims he can, but he can't."

"Who does that leave, Billy?"

"That fag."

Michele called, "What's happening with the drinks?"

All the glasses were dirty; no one in this group was interested in washing dishes. Shayne found some paper cups. Brownie was still pretending to read, to annoy Szigetti, but he put the book aside with relief when Shayne handed him a cup. There was a pile of newspapers beside him, and Shayne saw that afternoon's *World-Journal*. He kicked the pile over as he passed.

Michele mentioned food, and Szigetti made retching noises. "Don't make me throw up."

Shayne kept the former Marine supplied with whiskey and listened to another account of his adventures in the service. He rambled more and more as time passed. Forgetting where he was, he lapsed into a suspicious silence. His eyes rolled in his head, his head rolled on his shoulders. Finally the moment came, in the middle of the second bottle, when he didn't get his drink as far as his mouth and spilled it in his lap.

"Bedtime," Shayne said. "Big game tomorrow."

Szigetti objected, but he had come reeling to his feet to brush off the ice cubes, and the change of position finished him. Shayne steered him toward the door. They fell upstairs together. Shayne straightened the corridor out for him, picked him up when he fell down, and manhandled him into the bedroom he was using. On the approaches to the messy bed, Shayne released him and let him dive the rest of the way by himself.

Szigetti flopped over on the pillow, talking gibberish, as though his tongue was too large for his mouth and improperly attached. Then he fixed Shayne's swimming face in loose focus and said distinctly, "Miami. Bigshot detective. Whaz-name, Mike Shayne. Nev' mind, good buddy."

He smiled, his eyes whirled and he revolved himself asleep. Shayne turned and found Michele watching from the doorway.

If she had heard the name Mike Shayne, it meant nothing to her. "That was the quickest way, whiskey after whiskey, but oh, he will feel so sick tomorrow morning."

"Maybe sick enough to lay off Brownie. Let's see what we can find in the kitchen."

They found two minute steaks. Irene looked at the bloody, scored meat and turned pale. "It's whiskey on top of wine," she explained, and wobbled away, her fingers to her lips.

Brown and Billy were already gone. Michele cooked the steaks and they ate in the kitchen, under a glaring light. They left the dirty dishes on the table.

"What's your idea about the night?" Shayne said. "Separate rooms?"

"Positively! We have too many currents, *far* too many currents. Irene, for instance—it's clear that she fancies you, and if she thought we were asleep together she might steal in and murder us both."

"That's not the proposition she made me," Shayne said dryly.

They went up together and said goodnight at Michele's bedroom door. She kissed him silently and hurriedly.

"I wish I were in the habit of saying prayers. We need any help we can get."

Midnight, the time he had fixed on with Tim Rourke, had come and gone. In his own room, Shayne smoked a cigarette and finished the drink he had brought upstairs. He had to wait another half hour for everyone to settle down.

There was a faint scratching sound at the door. He turned off the light and waited, hoping that whoever it was would go away. The knob turned and the door opened slowly.

Billy's voice whispered, "Anybody awake?"

Shayne sighed and turned on the light. "Yeah." He went to meet the boy before he could get too far inside the room. "I'm beat, Billy. Some other time."

"I can't get to sleep," Billy said. "A couple of things bother me. I didn't want to ask *her*. I thought we could have a cigarette and talk for a few minutes."

"I wouldn't make any sense, kid. It's been a long day. Tomorrow after breakfast."

It took him five minutes to get rid of the boy without throwing him out bodily. He slid the bureau in front of the door and turned off the light again. He forced himself to wait ten minutes more. The last two minutes seemed to take almost as long as the first eight. He took the screen out of the window and swung out.

There was no light in Irene's bedroom. He eased himself slowly past. The night air was filled with the mating dialogue of small insects. A breeze stirred the branches of the overhanging maple, and one of the tree's spinning seeds hit him as he looked up.

Some of the tongue-and-groove lumber under the dry shingles had rotted away, but he decided that the two-by-six at the end of the roof, rotten or not, was going to hold him. He slid over and let himself down quickly. As soon as his feet touched the porch railing he let go and jumped to the ground.

The moon was in its final quarter, all but gone. He walked down the driveway without using the cover on either side. Approaching the gate, he moved more cautiously. He located the little electronic eye and stepped across.

He reached the crossroads out of breath after jogging most of the way. A dim neon glow still came from the bar and grill, but most of its customers had gone home for the night. Only three cars were parked on the pocked asphalt.

One was the same police Ford Tim Rourke had used during the day. Shayne crossed the parking area and got into the front seat with Tim and a girl.

CHAPTER 11

"You're overdue," Tim observed. "We just about gave you up. Cognac in the glove compartment."

The detective snapped open the little compartment, found the bottle and held it up to the light.

"We had a couple," Rourke said. "This is Terry Fox, Mike. She was out with Herman Kraus last night but she isn't sure she wants to talk about it. She let me put my arm around her so people would think we're necking, but that doesn't mean she thinks I'm a friend."

The girl stirred beside Shayne. "But who *are* you?" she said in a light, agreeable voice. "For a Miami newspaper reporter you're a long way from home. I don't know why I let you bring me all the way out here, except that those stories in the papers made me so damn *mad*."

Shayne unscrewed the cap of the bottle and drank. "I thought you would have explained things by now, Tim."

The reporter said hotly, "What do I know about what's going on? I came along with you because things always tend to happen where you're around. Just because I've already won one Pulitzer doesn't mean I'd mind winning another. I thought you'd talk about it on the plane, but you were too busy with those damn road maps. You have one infuriating habit, boy, and that's the way you hold up on explanations before you have everything wrapped up in tissue paper with all the ribbons tied. That's your method and most of the time, God knows, it seems to work. You told me to fall down and break a cackle bladder on my face, and did I ask any questions? Did I point out that I might have a hell of an embarrassing half hour if somebody found me before I could wash my face, which is the way it happened, incidentally?"

Shayne laughed. "If I'm still alive at the end of twenty-four hours, I'll sit down and give you the full play by play. Is it Miss Fox or Mrs.?"

"You might as well call me Terry," she said.

"All right, Terry. Do you think Kraus killed himself?"

"Of course he didn't."

She put a cigarette between her lips and pressed in the dashboard lighter. The faint glow showed Shayne a surprisingly pretty girl. She was younger than Herman Kraus, if the *News* had been right in giving his age as thirty-three.

"That's what I've been trying to tell people all day," she said, "and I haven't made an inch of headway. I'm furious! I'm so mad I could burst. The police won't talk to me, and still they put those lies in the papers. 'Spurned!' Herman wasn't spurned. I wasn't his fiancée. Tim says your name is Mike Shayne. Oddly enough, I heard Herman speak about you. He used to say he had no more to do with criminals than if he'd gone on working for an insurance company, which is where he started, and that's why he liked to read stories about real working detectives. I'm groggy, I'm afraid. You *are* the one he talked about?"

She reached behind him and snapped on the dome light. There were deep hollows in her cheeks, blue marks of weariness beneath her eyes. She remained an extremely pretty girl on the edge of exhaustion.

"You aren't at all! Mike Shayne has red hair."

Shayne flinched. "That's dye," he said in disgust.

"Does he or doesn't he?" Rourke murmured.

"Yeah. They tell me if I shampoo it with a strong enough soap it'll come right out. I'm under wraps on this, Terry."

She snapped off the light, and Shayne continued, "I see how you feel, and I wish I could give some answers. I don't know enough yet. But the cops had reasons for brushing you off today. There's something big in the works and they don't want to spoil it. They're hoping the fiancée story will hold up through the morning papers. They have a suicide note, it seems, a confession that your guy has been stealing narcotics."

"But that was over!" she exclaimed. "And he wasn't my guy!"

"You knew about it, Terry?"

"No, not really. But I've been doing some thinking today. I'm sorry to say that isn't something I make a practice of doing. Herman wasn't the major thing in my life, he really wasn't. I only saw him about once a week or once every two weeks—Well," she said philosophically, "there it goes, and I made up my mind when I agreed to come out here that I wouldn't say a word before I knew what you people are after."

"We're after the man who bankrolls the international heroin traffic," Shayne said. "I have doubts about a few stories I've heard lately, but I'm ninety-nine percent sure of that one thing. I think the chances are about even that I can get his identity. They're about one in four I can do anything about it even if I do find out. If you talk to me, it might drop the odds to something like seven-to-two."

"I can tell you this. Herman Kraus never had any connection with anybody in the international heroin traffic. He was way down at the bottom of the ladder."

"Yes, I think that's true, Terry," Shayne said seriously. "But whatever he did set something bigger in motion."

She rubbed her eyes, took a deep breath and exhaled a lungful of smoke. "When he left me last night we made a date for tomorrow, a specific date for a certain French movie at an art theatre. We agreed on where we were going afterward. Maybe it sounds conceited, but after that he didn't go straight home and shoot himself. That's what I've been trying to tell the police."

"Go back and tell it in order, Terry," Shayne suggested.

She drew on her cigarette. "I'll try to be honest. The reason I went out with him in the first place was because he put so much thought into where he would take me. He was a jerk, I'm afraid, but a perfectly harmless jerk. He'd call up and say he'd like to get tickets to some show I was dying to see, and I couldn't bring myself to say no. Then he'd take me to the Plaza or the Waldorf-Astoria or the Rainbow Room. This started about two years ago, when I was a lot younger than I am now. I wanted to see what those places were like! The other men I knew might take me to a party if they weren't expected to bring a bottle. If I had a date for a movie, we met inside. I felt a little—well, like a hypocrite, but I guess he had a good time because he always called me again. Once in a while I'd tell myself this has to stop. I knew I was getting in too deep. But by then I was worrying about hurting his feelings. He asked me to go to Saratoga Springs with him for the weekend. I went."

"Because you wanted to see Saratoga?"

"Yes! But it was a kind of obligation too, Mike. It's funny how things work out. Sometimes people I liked asked me to sleep with them or go away for the weekend and I wouldn't. But it seemed to me that I had to with Herman." She fumbled for a piece of Kleenex and blew her nose hard and angrily. "You wouldn't understand."

"I don't have to understand," Shayne told her. "People do things for the damnedest reasons."

"I might even have ended up married to him, just taking one step at a time. It makes me feel awful."

"Did you ever wonder where he was getting the money he spent on you, Terry?"

"He was spending it on himself too," she said with a flash of spirit. "*He* wanted to see those shows. *He* wanted to go to the Plaza. No, I didn't wonder. I didn't know about police salaries. He didn't talk about his work much, and I never once saw him in uniform. You didn't think of him as being a cop, somehow. And then quite a scary thing happened."

"When, Terry?"

"About two months ago. We were in a little bar—really a *tiny* bar. The tables were so big." She shaped a small square with her hands. "I don't remember where we'd been before—somewhere expensive! It was terribly noisy. I was chattering away, I do chatter, and Herman was trying to look interested. He probably couldn't hear what I was saying. And a man came up. He was honestly one of the creepiest people! Herman jumped up and told me he'd be right back. The bar was in a hotel, you could go in either from the street or the lobby. He went into the lobby. He *didn't* come back. There was some kind of commotion. A waiter said somebody'd been arrested. I went on sitting there, and he didn't come back at all. I barely had money enough to pay for the drinks. He called the next day and apologized for about fifteen minutes. He was always a great apologizer. He said the man he was talking to had a heart attack and he had to call an ambulance. I doubt that—I didn't hear an ambulance. And that's when I remembered all of a sudden that he'd said he was in charge of the evidence in dope cases. That man in the bar—he was on drugs, I realized. Well! Then I didn't see Herman for a few weeks. He said he had to work overtime. I wish I could be more helpful, Mike. I don't mean he was especially mysterious. He just didn't say what he was doing."

"You don't know how helpful you're being, Terry," Shayne said. "Go on."

"Helpful!" Rourke put in. "If you can make head or tail out of this you're a better man than I am. Well," he conceded, "you *are* a better man than I am."

Terry continued, "You might think I wouldn't go out with him again. I did, though. We were going to a film festival. We never got there. He drank too much before dinner and went to sleep in the taxi. If you think *that* had happened before! I took him home. In the morning he said he had something to tell me, but he felt too headachy and miserable, and I guess he didn't have much experience talking to people. He couldn't get started. The next time he was already high when he came to get me. I had the feeling he was drinking to get past that block, whatever it was, that kept him from talking. It made me uncomfortable. But last night was much better. My roommate was away. I didn't want to eat out because I knew he'd keep on ordering drinks in that stupid, compulsive way. I cooked spaghetti and everything was fine. He had a phone call during supper. He didn't say much except no, but he said it very firmly—it was as definite as he'd been in the two years I'd known him. Mike, could I have a drink, please?"

Shayne uncapped the bottle and gave it to her. The undiluted cognac made her cough.

"I'm glad I'm talking to you and not the police. They wouldn't give me cognac to help it along. Mike, I have something else that's important, at least I think it is. But you'll have to take it on faith, pretty much. We spent some time in my bedroom after dinner. This wasn't the accepted thing, it was always a big concession on my part. I never exactly looked forward to it. But last night he was different. It was"—there was a catch in her voice—"Mike, it was the best I've ever had with anyone. He'd stopped apologizing. Will you take my word for it and not ask any questions?"

"Sure."

"Maybe he was mixed up in something. You never can tell. I'd just like to see that so-called suicide note, that's all. The one thing I'm absolutely sure of is that, if he did shoot himself, it wasn't because I'd turned him down. The funny thing is, after last night I *could* have turned him down and I knew he wouldn't go to pieces. He'd changed into an actual grown-up person, finally."

Shayne finished the bottle and looked at his watch. He had to get back.

"Terry, one other question and don't feel bad if the answer is no. I want to know if he ever had contact with a French girl, a blonde, very elegant. I wish I could tell you the name of her perfume. You could probably identify her by it."

"Yes!" she said. "I don't know about the perfume, because that doesn't come over the phone. A girl called him at his apartment a week ago. I couldn't hear what she was saying, but there was something different about her voice, the few words I caught. All Herman did was mumble. He was very embarrassed."

Shayne thought for a moment. "I'm grateful for all this, Terry. The cops will probably be willing to listen to you tomorrow, but if you let it go another day you may not have to talk to them at all. Tim or I will be in touch."

Rourke cleared his throat gruffly. "I'll take that over. You'll have other things to do, Mike."

A grin formed on Shayne's lips, but he kept his voice level. "We can fight it out later."

Terry put her hand on his arm as he turned. "I'm still as much in the dark as I was, but I think I feel better. I've been so mad about everything all day I haven't had a chance to feel sorry about Herman. I don't know how much you charge, but if you can find out what happened to him—"

"I intend to," Shayne said, getting out. "But somebody else is paying my fee. Now go home and get some sleep."

"Yes, I think I can now."

CHAPTER 12

Somebody had left a light on in the kitchen, but the rest of the big house was dark and quiet. The people in it were apparently asleep. Shayne approached cautiously, hoping that the day was finally over and he, too, could get some sleep.

He stepped up on the porch rail. Reaching up with both hands, he got a grip on the overhang. A piece of rotten wood broke off. He shifted his hold, tested the new place for firmness, and committed himself to the upward spring.

His full weight was on the two-by-six for only an instant. Then he was over. He lay quietly, listening. The tree toads were still clamoring. He propelled himself forward on his elbows.

Irene's voice spoke clearly above him. "The tomcat returns."

He rolled over and sat up. The little moon threw just enough light to show that this was another member of the legion of girls who see no point in wearing anything to bed. Her jet-black shock of hair made a clear frame for the pale blur of her face.

"Why aren't you asleep?" Shayne said irritably. "You'll have bags under your eyes tomorrow."

"I had bags under my eyes when I was born," she said pleasantly. "I thought I heard you walking around, so I tried your door. And what do you know? There was a bureau against it."

"That was to keep Billy out, not you."

"Ha-ha. I never thought of climbing in the window.

Why don't I do that now? Then if anybody wants to interrupt, the bureau's in the way."

She put one bare leg out. Shayne grasped her ankle, but he wasn't able to stop her. She wasn't prepared for the pitch of the porch roof, and she came down on top of him.

"Ugh," she said. "It's all cindery."

"Irene, get back in your room and I'll come in with you. There's something I want to talk to you about."

"Who wants to talk? What I want to do—"

She put her mouth next to his ear and told him what she wanted to do, using the good old Anglo-Saxon expressions to make him realize she meant it.

"Yes, dear," he said, resigned. "You wouldn't consider waiting till tomorrow night, when we'd have more privacy?"

"No. I know you. You wouldn't show up. A bird in the hand is my motto." She drew back. "Where've you been, anyway? Out making a phone call?"

"Keep your voice down," he told her. "Climb back in and I'll tell you."

"Because I don't care," she said, and bit his ear. "But I've got you this time, haven't I, Tiger? Cooperate, or I'll tell Michele. It's OK with me if you call the cops, so long as I know about it in advance. I'm not that sold on this thing tomorrow. I'll just disappear ahead of schedule."

"Believe it or not," Shayne said patiently, "I was burying some money."

"And I don't believe it. You weren't listening to me—I don't *care*. Let's do it right here," she suggested. "Me on you."

One of her hands fumbled at him. Shayne tried to keep her under control, but it was like trying to control a marlin with boxing gloves, in the fish's own medium. He felt a board give way. He let go of the girl, twisting.

"You wouldn't want me to yell, would you?" she said dangerously. "I said cooperate. When you're going to be raped, you might as well relax and enjoy it. That's another old saying. And Buster, you are definitely going to be raped."

She was bearing down with her full weight. She was nothing but skin and bones, but at the moment much of the skin and all of the bones were in motion. Another board went. Then an entire section of the roof broke out beneath them.

Realizing what was happening, Irene kicked out for the window sill. The kick took out another rotting board. They went separate ways for a moment. Shayne's fingers closed briefly on the outer stringer, long enough to correct the angle of his fall. A post caved outward, the stringer broke, and Shayne and the naked girl went through to the porch beneath in a cascade of broken shingles and splinters of rotting wood. Shayne thought for an instant that he was going to keep on going. Irene landed in a hideous jangle of springs on a metal and chintz glider.

"Jesus," she said.

Shayne laughed. He tried to free her, but she was jammed in.

"Goddamn you," she said, "cut out that laughing and get a pair of pliers or something."

There were noises inside the house. A light came on in the living room, and then the porch light. Michele ran out, wearing only a slip. Brownie was right behind her, his muscular torso bare and gleaming. He had a shotgun.

"Somebody get me out of this thing!" Irene demanded. "Brownie! Use that shotgun—pry up the back."

"Here, baby," Shayne said. "I'll stand on it. See if it helps."

He stepped up on the swaying glider, one foot on each side of the stuck girl. The springs contracted. Moving carefully, Irene began to work herself free.

Michele came down on them like a sailboat in a stiff breeze, everything flying. She looked up at the gaping hole in the roof, then down at the naked girl jackknifed between the seat and the back of the glider. Shayne, bouncing gently, grinned at her.

"What does this mean?" she cried. "Tonight of all nights!"

Her English couldn't do justice to the situation, and she

broke into a flood of angry French. Irene came free with a little pop. She, too, had begun to think there was something funny about what had happened, but seeing Michele's face, she decided it was serious after all. Billy came out of the house, zipping his pants.

"Anybody hurt?" he asked, looking at Shayne.

"Which of you is to be the spokesman?" Michele said coldly. "Irene, dear? Were you trying to climb in his window?"

"Hell, no! The son of a bitch was trying to sneak out to phone. And phone who, I wonder?"

Shayne stepped off the glider. "If everybody will just keep quiet for a minute—"

Szigetti came charging out of the house. "What's going on?"

"That's what we all want to know," Shayne said. He started to take off his jacket. "Irene, baby, put this on. You'll catch cold."

She sniffed and marched into the house. It was a fair exit, Shayne thought, but she was too skinny; everybody continued to look at Shayne.

"You were about to explain," Michele said with icy sweetness. "Is what she says true? You were climbing out of the window to make a telephone call?"

"We better do this without an audience," Shayne said.

"Pardon me while I laugh," Szigetti sneered. "We're in this together, Jack. What's the story?"

The flesh around his eyes had puffed out so the eyes could scarcely be seen. They glinted suspiciously at Shayne within their pockets of gray flesh, but apparently he had forgotten identifying Shayne just before the tide of wine and whiskey had risen to engulf him.

"You're in bad shape, pal," Shayne observed as the smaller man swayed and reached for the doorway.

"I'll make it," Szigetti declared thickly. "Don't anybody go anyplace. Just get a drink."

"All the bottles are empty," Michele put in quickly. "You go back to bed, Ziggy. We handle this."

Szigetti glared at everyone in turn, ending with Brownie.

"And as for you, my shiny black friend—"

Compared to some of his earlier remarks this was nothing, but the Negro's composure finally snapped. He brought the shotgun barrels around and cracked Szigetti hard above the ear. Szigetti rocked. The glint in his eyes went out. Shayne caught him.

"Put him to bed, Billy. Anywhere."

Billy backed into the house with the unconscious gunman. Shayne jerked his head toward the lawn.

"Want me to cut out, Michele?" Brownie said.

She hesitated, then shook her head. "Stay here and keep the gun ready."

She followed Shayne down the steps.

"Now take it easy," he told her when they were out of hearing distance of the porch. "I tried to tell Irene, but she had other things she wanted to do besides listen. I had a last-minute errand. Remember those rocks I've been carrying around? I thought I better get rid of them."

"Get rid of them how?"

"What do you want me to do, draw a treasure map? I like you, baby. In fact I'm beginning to swing for you in a big way. But this is going to be my secret."

"Are you trying to tell me you *buried* them? You did nothing of the kind."

He said patiently, "Those stones are hot. If I get picked up tomorrow and the cops find anything like that on me I'll get the full treatment, and no last-minute reprieve."

She continued to look puzzled. "You left them in Grand Central with the money."

"I didn't leave anything in Grand Central," he said, still patient, "except an empty dispatch case. I know you think everybody ought to trust you, but look at it my way for a minute. A Grand Central locker, fine. Tomorrow, on the way to the plane, if there is any plane, all I have to do is detour a few blocks and pick it up."

"Of course there is a plane!"

"All right, there's a plane and we'll both be on it. So why did you get out of the car in front of Grand Central and follow me?"

"I was afraid," she said simply. "I did not think you saw me."

"You stick out in a crowd, baby. The back of my neck began to itch, and when that happens I always stop and think. These are nice friendly people you've got here, but there's one thing about them—they're all thieves. I'll be outnumbered tomorrow. I don't want to be jumped for that key. I couldn't carry it anyway, the cops would just match numbers and open the box. I'd have to stash it, so why not stash the dough and the stones instead? I brought it all back in the sack with the liquor."

"I think I do not believe you," she said with a sign of uncertainty. "Why climb out on the roof instead of just walking out by the back door?"

"I had the bureau in front of the door. Billy wanted to have a cigarette with me. I didn't want to have a cigarette with Billy." He took out the locker key and dangled it in front of her eyes. "The only way I can get in that locker without a key is to go to the office and describe my property. One cowhide dispatch case filled with cash, so much in hundreds, so much in fifties. Four unset diamonds in tissue paper. They used to belong to a character who got slapped on the head last night with a .45. Just before an ex-cop took two slugs in the body."

He went into a windup and sent the key spinning off into a tangle of alder and briers. He listened, but didn't hear it come down.

"It may be hanging from a twig where I can pick it up in the morning," he said. "And maybe not, too."

"I am sorry, darling," she said in a small voice. "This means we must come back here tomorrow?"

"If we're rushed we can leave it. It's in a safe place."

She gave a low laugh. "Why I was so angry was because of Irene. You are mine, dear, for the present. Please remember that."

He looked down at her for a moment. Then they turned and walked back to the house, arms touching.

CHAPTER 13

The Sanitation truck was scheduled to leave the police warehouse at ten-thirty. Because of the rechecking made necessary by the death of Herman Kraus, its departure was held up for an hour and three quarters.

Power had not been able to warn Shayne of the delay. The truck was due at the corner of Twenty-seventh Street and Sixth Avenue at eleven-ten. To be safe, Shayne's group had been in place fifteen minutes earlier. Except for Shayne himself, they became more and more conspicuous as the minutes passed. As for Shayne, he was wearing the uniform of the Sanitation Department, a little too tight, with an inspector's badge on his cap. He stood on the corner of Twenty-sixth with a clipboard, observing the traffic. He had a paper bag under one arm, containing, among other things, a .45 automatic. Occasionally, when a bus or a larger-than-usual truck went by on its way uptown, he made a small mark on a ruled pad that was clipped to the board. In the two hours he stood there, moving south to the corner of Twenty-fifth from time to time to break the strain, only one person paid any attention to him. This was a Puerto Rican boy, who watched for a time and then asked what he was doing.

"Making a survey," Shayne growled. "Beat it."

Szigetti was in a bar on the other side of the street, nursing a beer. A morning paper lay unopened beside him; he couldn't focus on anything smaller than a major headline. But he claimed to be ready for action in spite of his hangover, and to prove it, before leaving the house on Staten Island, he had gone down to his basement shooting gallery and put four out of six shots into the bull's-eye.

Irene, in a sliver of a luncheonette around the corner, was letting her sixth or seventh cup of coffee grow cold in front of her while she read the paper. That was all right; Shayne didn't think the name Herman Kraus would mean anything to her. Brownie was a short way up Twenty-sixth, at the wheel of a waiting car. On Twenty-seventh, his dress rack parked in the doorway of the nearest loft building, Billy was straddling a fire hydrant watching three or four neighborhood kids play stoopball.

At twelve-thirty Shayne used the glassed-in booth on the corner of Twenty-sixth to dial the number of one of the public phones in the Northwest terminal at LaGuardia. Michele answered.

"Still hasn't showed up," he said, rolling an unlighted cigar between his fingers. "How much longer do we wait?"

"Oh, God," she said. "There is a thing in the paper I don't like. Another few minutes."

"Baby," Shayne said softly, "we're out in the open here. What thing in what paper?"

He was able to imagine the expression on her face as she tried to decide how much to tell him. "A suicide. It frightened me at first, but it has no connection with us. It is because of a girl. It will make no difference."

"It better not make a difference," Shayne said roughly. "Because if somebody's blown this—"

"I'm sure it hasn't happened," she said quickly. "The story would be written in quite a different way."

"Baby—" Shayne began. He broke off, seeing Rourke's black Ford cruising slowly past. The left-turn blinkers were working, a signal that the garbage truck was four blocks away. "Here it is!"

He slammed down the phone. Coming out of the booth, he lit his cigar. He had been smoking cigarettes up to now. Brownie, seeing the lighted cigar, switched off the motor of the car he was in and came out onto the street. In the luncheonette, Irene got up hastily with a nervous yawn, giving her bangs a pat. As Shayne came abreast of the bar, Szigetti appeared in the doorway, blinking and loosening his shoulders, seeming to be fighting off a wave of nausea.

Shayne had to whistle to Billy. The boy jumped up and ran for the dress rack. On Twenty-seventh, a small man whose name Shayne hadn't been told cranked up a tractor and began to jackknife his trailer out into the working lanes, preparing to close off the block.

Shayne crossed to the west side of Sixth as the Sanitation truck came into view, a lumbering monster painted bright yellow, with the Department of Sanitation insignia on the door and over the high cab. Traffic was moving smoothly. The sidewalks were jammed with garment workers on lunch hour. Billy worked his rack through the knots of gossipers on the sunny corner. He reached the utility post while the garbage truck was between Twenty-fifth and Twenty-sixth.

The lights were synchronized so that a theoretical single car, moving at a steady thirty-three miles an hour, could drive from one end of the island to the other, meeting nothing but green lights all the way. In real life, of course, nothing is so simple. Cars move in packs. Midday traffic jams in this district were common. Billy reached up to the one-way arrow on the lamp post and waited. The truck passed Szigetti. Billy pressed the button.

Surprised, for he expected a few more blocks on the green, the driver came down on his brakes and stopped with his front wheels over the pedestrian line.

The big trailer near the Broadway end of the short block slanted across the street. It continued to maneuver forward and back, not leaving enough space for anything to get by. The cars on the Sixth Avenue side of the blockade began to move on the green.

Shayne stepped off the curb as Irene ran screaming along the opposite sidewalk, with Brownie right behind her. In rehearsals they had timed this entire segment of the action at under thirty seconds. The Sanitation truck had two sets of handgrips on the tailgate, one on each side of the conveyor belt which carried trash and garbage to the powerful chopper which chewed it up before letting it drop into the main bin. Two cops were clinging to the handgrips, their heads turned toward the sidewalk.

The moment Shayne stepped off the curb, Billy rolled the dress rack along the sidewalk to Szigetti. Turning on his heel, he started back up Twenty-seventh.

Irene screamed, "No! Don't! Let me alone, damn you!"

These were not the lines she had rehearsed; she believed in the spontaneous school of acting. There was no doubt, Shayne thought, that to an onlooker her terror and revulsion were real. Brownie overtook her and yanked her around. He gave her a slap that sent her staggering back against a parked car. She caromed off and came back with her fingers raised and curled.

"Don't do that again, Sambo!" she warned. "Your white-pussy days are over. Get back uptown where you belong, black boy!"

Brownie seized her long black hair. "Where you been these last two nights? You cheated on me for the last time, you ofay bitch!"

He worked up a mouthful of spit and released it in her face. A sound came from the crowd. She slowly wiped the spit out of her eyes while Brownie collected another mouthful.

One of the cops jumped down and shouted to the driver, "Wait here!" After an instant's hesitation the second cop joined him, feeling for his nightstick.

Still holding Irene's hair in his fist, Brownie backed her across the sidewalk, his face only a few inches from hers. The sudden violence had emptied a patch of sidewalk around them.

"Who's going to make me go?" he yelled. "Not you, Whitey! Not by yourself! Better bring a few friends!"

Whirling her by the hair, he slammed her against the window of a shoe-repair shop. She tried to knee him in the groin. Both cops started across the sidewalk, their night-sticks half-raised.

Shayne reached the cab. He wrenched the door open and snapped, "Move over. Street's blocked up ahead."

The driver took in Shayne's uniform and badge in a

glance and began to move. His companion was craning out the other window.

"Big colored fellow beating up on a white girl!" he cried excitedly.

Szigetti slid the dress rack into the open space between the cops and the quarreling lovers. He pushed hard. They batted foolishly at the swinging dresses, as Shayne had done two nights before in the house on Staten Island. While they were tied up, Szigetti reached through the dresses and squirted tear gas into their eyes from a pocket dispenser.

Irene and Brownie had already separated and disappeared.

Szigetti screamed, "Where'd that black bo go? He threw acid at them! Come on!"

He raced into a nearby vestibule, but no one else in the crowd wanted to join him in the pursuit of a large, dangerous Negro who had already managed to disable two cops. The cops were clawing at their eyes.

Above in the truck's high cab, Shayne jammed the stick into low and was off with a roar, swinging the wrong way into Twenty-seventh. Both lanes ahead were empty. So far Michele's scheme was working well.

"One-way street!" the regular driver cried.

"Don't I know it," Shayne said grimly, chewing on his cigar. "Some jokers are trying to hijack us. Not if I have anything to say about it."

The driver Shayne had displaced was a small, swarthy man, and like Shayne he had a cigar between his teeth. He hadn't been told what cargo he was carrying. All he knew was that the cartons and canvas bags had been loaded with care, being checked off one by one on a master list as it was put in the truck. Instead of using the rear hatchway and the conveyor belt, they had been loaded through the side hatch, so they could be rechecked at the incinerator. And then he had been given a two-cop escort, another indication that something unusual was happening.

After one look at Shayne, he peered worriedly ahead at the trailer truck. It inched forward, leaving just enough room for a scooter or a Volkswagen to squeeze past.

Shayne slowed. Billy burst from between two parked cars and leaped onto the foothold on the right of the cab. Clinging to the door handle he yelled, "In there! Take a right! A right! For Christ's sake give her some gas!"

Shayne swung the wheel hard. The big truck rocked up over the curb. At the sight of the wooden police barrier Shayne hit the brakes. Billy screamed and he bulled ahead. The barrier went over and was crushed beneath the front wheels.

He plunged into the alleyway he and Michele had reconnoitered the day before. Behind the building he veered sharply into the unloading space. Billy threw the door open on his side, waving a gun.

"Out!" he shouted. "You guys out!"

The Sanitation worker nearest him was slow to move. Billy jabbed him in the ribs.

"I said move!"

The regular driver looked at Shayne, his black eyes liquid with terror.

Shayne said warily, "I don't know about you, but I've got kids. Let's let somebody else be a hero."

"All of you!" Billy said, his voice high.

The two Sanitation workers slid past Billy onto the loading platform. Shayne followed, his hands raised.

"Lie down," Billy snapped.

The two men fell obediently to their knees. Billy whipped out handcuffs. He had four pairs, two of which he tossed to Shayne.

"Hands behind you," he told the Sanitation men.

So far Shayne had been following Michele's schedule. Now for the first time he introduced one of the variations he had worked out with Power. A burly plainclothes detective, garbed as a janitor, came out of the loft building, carrying a mop and a ten-quart pail filled with dirty water. Billy was stooping over the driver, putting the handcuffs on his ankles. He looked around as the janitor swung the pail, knocking him sprawling. The detective then hit him with the mop and dived for his gun hand. Billy managed to free the gun, but the detective, working with speed and precision,

115

brought Billy's arm down sharply across the edge of the loading platform. The gun dropped to the blacktop below.

Shayne hit the detective a token blow, and the detective staggered backward, sitting down hard. Billy wrenched himself up and fell on him.

"Go on!" Billy cried over his shoulder at Shayne. "Go!"

The detective was flopping around, pretending to be trying to free himself. Shayne hesitated.

Billy shouted again and Shayne leaped into the cab. He let the truck's acceleration slam the door for him. He headed for the dividing wall on the property line, and hit it squarely. Sure enough, it went down with a clang.

Through another delivery alley, almost a continuation of the one he had just left, he saw Twenty-eighth Street. There was another wooden barrier at the mouth of the alley. Being in less of a hurry now, he removed it by hand, and turned east on Twenty-eighth.

At Broadway he stopped following the route that had been laid out for him. The excavation site where the cargo was to be transferred was on Twenty-first, seven blocks downtown. He turned uptown on Fifth. At the Empire State Building he turned left, staying on Thirty-fourth as far as Eleventh Avenue.

At this point he pulled in to the curb, raised the hood and removed three spark plugs. After prying up the points so they would no longer fire, he put them back and slammed down the hood.

The engine took hold haltingly and he went into the Sanitation Department Motor Shop on five cylinders.

One long wall of the shop was lined with big yellow trucks waiting for repairs. Two mechanics were working on a truck without a front wheel. There were other workmen around the grease pit in back. A small man in oil-spattered overalls came out of a little office and listened while Shayne raced the motor.

"Could be a bearing," he said. "Pull in over there."

Shayne maneuvered the truck into an open space in the rank, shut off the motor and came back to the office. The official wrote down the truck's serial number and the name Shayne gave him, which was that of the regular driver.

"How soon can you go to work on her?" Shayne said.

"Christ, look at the jobs we got lined up. Maybe next week."

Shayne nodded indifferently. Outside, he tossed his cigar away, shut himself in a phone booth and dialed the La-Guardia number.

Michele answered promptly.

"What do you think," Shayne said. "Trouble."

"Trouble! Ziggy said everything was fine. Where are you?"

"Stop asking questions and listen. It may still be OK. I think I broke the gas line when I went over that fence. Gas all over the street. Now here's the thing. A guy I know has a truck and he'll be here in a minute. We'll transfer the load on the street. I've got the uniform on. Nobody'll bother us. If the son of a bitch only hurries."

Michele forced herself to be calm. "And you will drive from there to Twenty-first Street?"

"Hell, no. We're going to be hearing the sirens in a couple of minutes. I want to get all the way out of the neighborhood. And they got Billy. He knows the Twenty-first Street address, so better call them and tell them to clear the hell out."

"I wait here."

"No, go to your apartment. There's my guy now. Yeah. Now don't worry about him, he's OK—There's the siren!"

"But—"

He slammed down the phone, grinning.

CHAPTER 14

He had checked his suitcase at Pennsylvania Station. He changed into his new suit in the men's room and checked his appearance in the mirror. The men in the Brooks Brothers cutting rooms had allowed for all the usual possibilities, but they hadn't expected any of their customers to wear a shoulder holster under one of their suits. There was a definite wrinkle.

He hung the Sanitation Department uniform in a cleaning closet, and put the suitcase into another coin locker. After paying his way into the subway, he studied the map and decided on the Eighth Avenue uptown express. The train he wanted pulled in a moment later. The trip took only a few minutes. Michele's apartment was several blocks from the subway station, and Shayne walked rapidly. He wanted to be the first to arrive.

He picked his way into the inner lobby, using the small set of burglar's tools which he carried wherever he went. Ascending to the twelfth floor, he rang the bell at 12-H. There was no answer.

He lit a cigarette, looked at his watch thoughtfully and went back down the hall to the door of the incinerator. This was a small closet with a bin in the inner wall facing the door. The landlord, an aluminum company, had posted a notice telling tenants what articles not to throw down the chute. Shayne ripped the notice off the wall and scrawled across its back: "Out of Order Use Incinerator on 11th Floor." He punched a hole in the cardboard and hung it on the outer doorknob. Then he shut himself in.

A few minutes later a woman's high heels clicked toward the incinerator. A voice said wearily, "Oh, the bastards," and the heel-clicks went to the elevator. An elevator picked her up and in another moment brought her back. She returned to her apartment.

Shayne went on waiting.

The next time the elevator stopped at that floor he heard Michele's voice, low and guarded.

"He may be already here, so be careful."

When footsteps passed, Shayne cracked the door and looked out. He saw Michele, in the stylish suit she was wearing today. She had Brownie with her. She motioned to Brownie to stand so he couldn't be seen through the one-way peephole, and slid a key into the lock. *"Merde,"* she said. It was the wrong key.

Shayne opened the door and stepped out, the .45 in his hand. Two long strides ate up half the intervening space. Brownie whirled, his hand stabbing toward his jacket.

"Hold it, Brownie!" Shayne snapped. "This isn't Russian roulette. I'm carrying a full clip. Hi, baby," he said to Michele. "I thought you might pick up somebody on the way in. Now I want both of you to do this my way. Don't panic. It's going to cost you some money, but I've got everything under control."

"Darling!" Michele cried. "Why should I not bring somebody? We could not handle it alone, the two of us."

Shayne grinned savagely. "Couldn't we? Brownie, turn around. Keep your hands out where I can see them. Open the door slowly. Very slowly."

She put the key in the right lock and did as he told her, after a puzzled glance at the .45. Inside, they bunched up in the little foyer. Shayne kicked the door shut. He disarmed Brownie, touching the small of his back with the .45 while he went inside Brownie's coat to get the pistol in his waistband.

Shayne herded the French girl into the kitchen space and handcuffed her to the door of the refrigerator, using one of the two pairs of handcuffs that had been meant for the driver of the Sanitation truck.

"My God," she said.

"What the hell'd you expect?" Shayne burst out. "Do you know what that truck was carrying?" he asked Brownie. "Junk! Heroin, coke, reefers—you name it. Cartons of the stuff. And that makes a difference, kid," he said, touching Michele's shoulder lightly with his gun. "OK, Brownie. We're going for a walk."

"Nobody told me!" Brownie cried. "All I got so far is five bills. I'm with you, man. Anything you say."

"The first thing to do is shut up," Shayne told him.

Sweat had broken out on Brownie's forehead. "OK," he whispered. "What do I care?"

Shayne jerked his head toward the door. He locked the bolt in the open position and flicked the spring lock so he could get back in without a key. Brownie walked down the hall ahead of him, taking deep breaths as though each one was his last.

"Right here," Shayne told him at the door of the incinerator.

"I really didn't know about it," Brownie said. "This is funny as hell."

"Cheer up, Brownie. With a little luck you'll live through it."

"Luck," Brownie said bitterly. "I don't know the word."

Shayne took out the second pair of handcuffs. Brownie was glad to see them, having expected Shayne to use the .45. In a moment he was handcuffed to the incinerator bin.

"I put an out-of-order sign on the door," Shayne said. "Keep quiet and maybe nobody'll know you're here. Hijacking a cargo of horse is serious, man, thirty years to life. If I happen to think of it, I'll come back tonight with a hacksaw."

"I'll appreciate it," Brownie said simply.

Shayne removed the bullets from Brownie's .38 and dropped the unloaded weapon down the chute. He took the rounds with him; live ammunition was one of the things the landlord didn't want tenants to put in the incinerator.

Back in Michele's apartment, he locked the door and stood for a moment smiling at her. She returned his gaze coolly.

"I had a faint hope that you would not look in the cartons," she said.

"Do you know I damn near didn't? I could see it was police evidence, the way you said, and blackmail crap is something I wouldn't know how to handle. But this stuff is as good as cash."

"Not quite. You need a buyer you can trust."

"You're my buyer," he said. "Not that I better start trusting you this late in the day."

"I admit I lied to you, but it was necessary. You would never have done it otherwise."

"How right you are, not for a lousy fifteen G's. There's going to be some real heat. If I didn't have you as a contact, I'd find a nice deserted pier and dump the damn stuff."

"You would not."

He shrugged. "Wouldn't I?"

He went into the other room for the bourbon and poured himself a drink.

"Nothing for me, I see," she commented.

He ignored the remark. After tasting the whiskey he sat down where he could watch her, and lit a cigarette. She hooked a stool with her toe and pulled it close enough to the refrigerator so she could perch on it.

"Seriously," she said.

"OK, I'll be serious. What can I do with this load, open a store? I'm not in the business, and frankly it scares me. And this buddy of mine with the truck. It's registered in his right name, and that means we have to get it out of that truck fast. I guess I wouldn't dump it in the river, at that. I'd dump it in Central Park and set it on fire. If you want it, you've got till eleven tonight."

"What is your price?"

"Five hundred grand."

Her eyebrows went up, and her lips formed a tiny O.

"And don't try to beat me down," he said, blowing out smoke. "I like those nice round numbers. I happen to know how much H is retailing for now per ounce. I made a guess at how many ounces. Ounces, hell. Tons. It's a fair price. You still ought to clear about a million bucks. That's OK with me. You have the setup to merchandise it. I don't."

She smiled. "You expect me to believe there is no place you would settle between nothing and a half million?"

"There's an easy way to find out," Shayne said. "Say no and I won't have to wait till tonight."

"Do you know," she said after a moment, "I think you would actually do it."

Shayne went on smoking in silence, his eyelids hooded.

She said, "If I ask you very nicely, may I have a drink?"

He got a glass, pushed the bottle within her reach and let her pour it herself with her free hand. She tossed it off and thought for a moment. She said decisively, "I suppose my answer must be yes. Unlock me."

"I don't have the key."

She gave him a startled look. "I do not carry half a million dollars in my purse, after all."

Shayne went on smoking. "You're the genius. Suggest something."

"Darling," she said. "Do you still consider coming to Europe with me?"

Shayne looked at her bleakly. "Why? Before you give me a half million, you want to know if we're going to end up with a joint checking account?"

She smiled slightly. "Something like that. A joint account—no, that would be going too far. If you wish, you can go somewhere and live like a cinema star until the money is gone. Las Vegas, now there is the logical place. Sit down in a casino with a roll of thousand-dollar bills. The girls will notice you, the police will notice you, the income tax people will notice you. And very soon you will be without money again, if not in prison. Why not change your way of doing these things, darling? You could do worse than throw in with me. It is a practical proposal. The plane is waiting. I do not press you to say for certain. Merely think about it."

"You go on ahead," Shayne said with a trace of a grin. "I'll join you later."

Now there was a frightened look in her eyes; she clearly wasn't accustomed to having her proposals rejected. She gave a slight shrug.

"Very well. The money. I promise to pass on your figure, but I can tell you now, a half million dollars on demand is out of the question. Time will have to be given, thirty days at least, so some of the drugs can be sold."

Shayne shook his head. "It has to be cash. I don't give a damn how you raise it. That's your business."

"Half a million!" she said scornfully. "One hundred thousand, perhaps one twenty-five." As he made a move to get up, she added hastily, "I act as messenger. How will you make delivery?"

Shayne rubbed the side of his jaw. "I'll let you know. I'm going to need another truck, to begin with." A smile spread over his face. "One of those Sanitation jobs—why not? I've still got the uniform. The bigger they are, the easier they are to steal. I'll take a room at that motel we were in yesterday. I want to get a phone call at four, and I do mean on the dot. I don't insist on small bills, but nothing over a hundred. This buddy of mine is in the building business, and he's going to get me a blasting cap. You know what they are. I'll rig it to a jug of gasoline. I know I won't have time to count the full half million. Even with nothing smaller than hundreds I couldn't wade through it in less than half an hour. Maybe an hour—I have no idea at all. What I want you to do is have them set it up in ten packages, fifty thousand apiece. I'll check a couple at random. Now I want you to be sure you've got the picture, baby. This Molotov cocktail will be planted in the truck. I'll carry the detonator in the palm of my hand." He leaned forward, his eyes intent on hers. "Don't short-count me, kid. Don't anybody try to jump me. If I so much as *smell* trouble, if that count is off by more than a few hundred—"

He closed his fist on the glass and it shattered in his

hand. He held her eyes for a moment more, and then laughed.

"That's making a point the hard way." He threw the pieces of broken glass into the sink. "So long as you remember, that detonator's going to be the only protection I'll have."

"You keep surprising me. That is actually rather intelligent, and I mean to pass it on. I keep coming back to what happens then."

"Give me a number to call and I'll tell them to come and get you."

"I would rather have you come and get me."

Shayne had cut the palm of his hand. He wadded up a dish towel and clenched it in his fist to stop the bleeding.

"What kind of a plane have you got?" he said.

"A Jetstar. Captain and navigator."

"Who's it registered to?"

"A certain company in Luxembourg. If you have something against Portugal, the captain will drop us off wherever we wish en route. Cuba. The Bahamas. Tangier. If you wish to believe I am thinking primarily of the money, believe it. It may even be true. Does it matter? I am considerably taken with you, my dear. Is absolute trust necessary between two people? Of course not. I keep my eye on you, you keep your eye on me. If we are in bed together much of the time, that will be easy."

Shayne shook his head admiringly. "Don't you ever give up? Well, I have the afternoon to think about it."

"I make progress," she said. "Come a bit closer. Have you ever made love to a girl chained to a refrigerator?"

Shayne grinned. "How can you think of sex when there's a half million dollars at stake? And don't tell me it's the same thing."

He went for the phone. It was on a table at the end of the sofa. The cord only stretched as far as the edge of the kitchen area. She reached for it, but there was still a gap of several feet.

"That settles it, surely," she said. "You will have to cut

124

me loose. There is a hardware store on Amsterdam Avenue where you can get a saw."

"And then what?" Shayne said. "I don't have any more handcuffs. Give me the number and I'll do the talking."

"No. Because then you could bypass me, and I would be left out in the cold. I must dial the number, at least. In the drawer there, beside the sink. A sharpener for the meat knife."

Shayne sorted through the drawer and brought out a bone-handled implement with an abrasive surface and a round end. He put the phone on the floor. Michele found that by reaching out at her full stretch, she could fit the end of the sharpener into the holes of the dial.

"You agree this is a reasonable request?" she said.

"Go ahead and dial the goddamn number."

He went into the other room, making no attempt to see what number she was painstakingly dialing. What she didn't know was that Power had inserted a device in the base of the phone to record the numbers of outgoing calls.

She called Shayne back and told him, "Ask for extension thirty-eight."

He picked up the phone. In a moment a girl's voice said hello.

"Thirty-eight," Shayne said.

"Thirty-eight? Are you sure you have the right—oh, yes. One moment."

Then a man's voice said pleasantly, "Yes?" It was the same voice Shayne had heard when he tapped the Staten Island line.

"I'm a friend of a friend," Shayne said. "You may not want to mention any names."

"Nonsense, why not? This friend would be Michele?"

"Yeah. You may not worry about your phone, but I think I'll worry about mine. So you'll know who's talking, she paid me seven and a half G's yesterday, and she owes me another seven and a half."

"Making fifteen in all," the voice said, amused.

Shayne grunted. "I thought she cut a piece for herself before it got as far as me. If anybody ever gives this doll the lie-detector test, she'll wreck the machine. Well, you probably know by now that things have gone a little sour."

"But not totally, I understand? Where is Michele?"

"Right here, but she can't come to the phone." He lowered his voice, holding Michele's eyes across the intervening space. "You probably want to know what it's going to cost you. Five hundred thousand."

"How much?" the voice said sharply, losing its pleasant quality.

"An even half million. In American money. That's not the asking price, it's the ticket on the deal. I've just been arguing with her, and I think I've convinced her I mean it. Of course she's hoping to siphon some of it her way sooner or later. How long will it take you to scrape up that much cash?"

"It can't be done in any amount of time. I don't have it."

"Do your best," Shayne said philosophically. "I want to give you a phone number." He thumbed through the yellow pages for the number of the motel, and read it off. "Call me there at four and I'll tell you the next step. Ask for Matt Maguire. If I don't get that call, I'm setting fire to the truck. Which would be a shame, considering all the dough you've already put into this."

"You're bluffing. Nobody bluffs me. I was about to make you a more realistic offer. But if that's the way you want it—"

Shayne interrupted. "That's the way I want it. Don't try to play poker with crazy people. I'm nuts, I admit it. I don't like handling junk. Neither do you, I notice, whoever the hell you are. They murder you on a drug rap in this state. I'll deal with you for five hundred grand and not a penny less. Michele knows me. Michele, baby, tell the man. Will I set fire to the truck if I keep getting this price-is-too-high routine?"

He held out the phone.

"Yes," she said.

"Louder," Shayne told her. "Say something else so he'll know it's really you."

"Yes, Mr. A.," she said, "he really will."

"Put her on," the man's voice said.

Shayne laughed. "Huh-uh. I'm just a country boy, but I know if I'm not careful with you guys I'll lose my teeth. Think about it for another thirty seconds."

"It is two o'clock now. You are allowing me two hours to raise the money. I doubt that it's enough. You know nothing about how business is conducted in the modern world."

"But this isn't a regular business, is it? That reminds me. If you're thinking about sending some muscle to the motel to beat my head in, don't. I've parked the stuff with a friend of mine, and he's itchier than I am. If I don't call him by five after four, whoosh!"

"I see," the voice said softly. "I think I understand the situation. Till four."

Shayne hung up. "How old is he, anyway?" he asked Michele.

"Older than you," she told him, "and far less interesting."

"I'll bet," Shayne said dryly.

He moved the phone well beyond her reach, and tossed off a fast drink. Michele continued to watch him.

"If you try," she said, "you can think of some better way than leaving me chained to a refrigerator."

"It won't be so bad," Shayne said. "If you get hungry, you've got everything right there. In one way I'd like to wait till dark, but I think I'll need daylight for this transfer. It's going to be touch and go there for a couple of minutes. I'll try to get everything wound up by five, and let's hope for your sake it goes off OK. The last thing I'll say to the guy will be where he can find you."

"Perhaps you will decide to come yourself, after all."

Shayne grinned. "I'll keep thinking about it."

He brushed his hand across her breast, and her lips parted. He took her keys and threw the bolt from the outside. On the way to the elevator he opened the door of the incinerator closet and told Brownie, "Everything's rolling right along."

CHAPTER **15**

Power had been waiting for Shayne's call. He answered instantly.

"I wish you'd consider opening a New York office," Power said jubilantly after Shayne reported what had happened. "Could we use a man like you around here! All right. I don't want to take any unnecessary chances. I'm still not persuaded that Kraus was their only man in the department, so let's play it close to the vest. You, me, Tim Rourke and Jamieson—the four of us ought to be able to handle it. Tim can operate the camera. This is one arrest I think I deserve to make in person."

"I only see one hole in it," Shayne said thoughtfully. "If this guy is strictly a money man, why won't he send somebody to make delivery? The way he sounded, he's not somebody who sticks his neck out unless he has to, and it doesn't seem to me he has to."

"You may be right," Power conceded. "But this is no ordinary deal, and would he trust anybody else with it? A half million in cash—that's a powerful temptation. Even so. He'll have to do his own recruiting this time, and that's going to give us one more link. We can get the phone number from the girl's phone. Extension thirty-eight will pinpoint it. We have the girl herself, or we will have. We have a lead to the bank on William Street. I think it may be nearly enough."

"Maybe," Shayne said dubiously. "What do I tell him when he says he can't raise the full half million? Do I settle for less?"

"Play it by ear, Mike. The one thing you really have to

convince him of is that you'll blow up the truck at the first hint of trouble. That's essential. They lock up the Motor Shop at four. Get down there as fast as you can. It shouldn't take more than five minutes to set up. I'll bring everything we need. Give him a five-o'clock deadline—he'll need that long to package the money. I've got a hunch we're going to put this over, Mike."

"I hope so."

He hung up, troubled by something too vague to be called a premonition.

He checked in at the motel. Alone in his room, he found a ball game on TV, took off his jacket and tie and sat back against the head of one of the twin beds with a glass in one hand and a pint of cognac within reach. He went over the plan again. Something continued to pick at him, but he wasn't able to chase it down. They had set up a tight schedule, leaving the opposition too little time to work out any counterplan. There were three things that could happen, and as far as Shayne could tell, no more than three. If the banker appeared in person, they would film the transaction and have the most important narcotics arrest of the decade. If he sent an agent, they would still have an important arrest, as well as a fair case against the man at the top if they could find him. As for number three, if the banker decided not to believe Michele's evaluation of Shayne and to take a chance that he was bluffing, a quick reflex action on Shayne's part would destroy the truckload of drugs there on the street instead of at the Sanitation Department's incinerator. Everything seemed to be covered. And yet—

His eyes fixed on the TV picture without really seeing it, he started over, and again he failed to find the loophole he was sure was there. The minute hand on his watch worked slowly around. He was still dissatisfied when the phone rang during the four-o'clock station break.

"Maguire?" the familiar voice said.

"Yeah," Shayne said, swinging off the bed. "Could you make it?"

"Not quite. I have four hundred and twenty thousand."

"Too bad," Shayne said shortly. "Hang up. I want to use the line."

There was a brief pause.

"Five hundred then," the voice said in a resigned tone. "Where do we make the exchange?"

Shayne told him, then went on to give instructions on how he wanted the money packed. He gave a detailed description of the way the truck would be wired, as a precaution against treachery.

"So make sure you do it all by yourself," he said. "You'll recognize me. I'll be leaning against the front fender smoking a cigar. I'll leave the motor running. All you have to do is put it in gear and go. You do know how to drive, I hope."

"One of those immense rubbish vans? Don't be childish. Make a different arrangement, or I'll have to bring a driver."

"No," Shayne said. "You can have a driver waiting at the corner of Tenth Avenue, but the transfer has to be strictly one to one. Take off the hand brake and put her in low. It's right where it is on any manual shift. Stay in low till you get to Tenth."

"Perhaps," the man said with a sigh. "I won't claim to be glad our paths have crossed, Mr.—Maguire, but I'm impressed, as always, with American speed and ingenuity. Do you care to tell me where you've secreted Michele?"

"I'll tell you after you hand over the dough."

"You made quite an impression in that quarter, it seems. Too bad. It might have worked out to your advantage."

He hung up, and Shayne moved fast. He went out carrying his tie and jacket, and put them on waiting for the elevator. A cab took him downtown on Ninth Avenue and let him out in front of the Department of Sanitation Motor Shop at four-sixteen.

The big overhead doors were down. He knocked on a smaller door. Inspector Power opened it almost at once.

"Did he agree, Mike?"

"We're getting the full price," Shayne said, "and I think he's bringing it himself. This could pay off."

"It's about time something broke right for our side," Power said. "Let's change the plugs."

The big yellow truck Shayne had brought in was easy to pick out of the deadlined vehicles because of a bad dent he had put in its front fender by knocking down the iron fence. After replacing the three spoiled spark plugs, he swung into the cab and started the motor. It took hold with a roar. He pulled onto the floor, where Power was waiting with two one-gallon jars of kerosene.

"You'll want to be sure of the connections, Mike. Open the side hatch."

Shayne threw the heavy clamps. The side door swung open. The space inside was crammed with cartons, canvas bags and bundles of nine-by-twelve manila envelopes, tied with twine. He flipped one of the cartons open and pulled out an envelope. All the necessary information about the case of one John Gonzales, arrested two summers earlier for possession of narcotics, was entered on the front of the envelope in a careful clerk's hand: the police code number, the name of the arresting officer, a listing of the evidence and the disposition of the case. Gonzales, seized with a broken eyedropper and eleven one-ounce bags of heroin, had pleaded guilty. Unless he had been paroled in the interim, he was still in jail.

Shayne shook one of the innocent-seeming glassine packages into his hand. He tossed the envelope back with the rest and shook his head.

"What a haul."

"Here, Mike, put it as far in back as you can reach."

Power passed up one of the jars of kerosene. A blasting cap had been fitted into the lid and sealed there with paraffin. Shayne paid out the wire carefully and wedged the jar into a nest of cartons.

"One would probably be enough," Power said, "but let's not take any chances."

He handed up the second jar, identical with the first. Shayne placed it and jumped down. Power closed the hatch gently, leaving it unlatched so it wouldn't pinch the wires.

The detonator was already tied in. Shayne took it into the cab with him.

Power pressed a button activating the overhead doors. Shayne drove through, parked pointing east and left the motor idling. The gas gauge was three-quarters full.

Power lowered the big door and came out by the small one. His movements were as deliberate as usual, but Shayne could see excitement in his eyes.

"That detonator. You know how to work it, Mike? Give the crank a couple of turns. There's a safety latch, and you've got to give it a real hard push. Tim Rourke's in a panel truck on the other side of the street. Jamieson's in with him. Tim's the only one who can see out, but all he has to do is say the word and Jamieson'll jump. Try to work your man so they get a good picture of his face. Where do you think you ought to count the money?"

"Up in the cab would be the best place."

Power nodded. "Just don't push the plunger while you're in there. I think the body is strong enough to contain it, but just the same." He glanced at his watch. "Four-twenty-three. Not bad." He looked at Shayne, liking and respect for the big private detective obvious on his lined face. "We'll have a few snorts together when this is over."

Shayne gave him a crooked grin. He leaned back against the dented fender and lit a cigar. Power went into the lobby of the next building. After a moment Shayne turned idly to look for Rourke's panel truck. It was a battered maroon and white International, to all appearances a bakery delivery truck. The aperture for the camera lens was well concealed. Even knowing what to look for, Shayne couldn't spot it.

The detonator was roughly the size of a cigar box. Shayne had it in a paper bag, holding it loosely in his left hand. After cranking the handle of the plunger, he was ready. Anyone who looked closely could have seen two wires coming out of the bottom of the bag, running down to the gutter and from there to the side hatch; but Shayne already knew that this was a city where people minded their own business. A block from the waterfront, there were few pedestrians, most of them looking like longshore-men or teamsters. Three out of four of the vehicles turning in from Eleventh Avenue were trucks.

Shayne's big body was relaxed, his eyes sleepy, but in fact he was as alert as a terrier watching a woodchuck hole. The motor of the big truck ticked behind him. Trouble, he knew, could come from any direction. Power covered him on one side, Jamieson on the other, but he was relying mainly on the detonator, and he kept the paper bag in plain view.

He smoked his way through two cigars. He was in the middle of the third when the big rearview mirror on the truck's fender showed him a man in a black Homburg and a well-cut dark suit, which made him conspicuous in that neighborhood. Shayne came around without hurrying, his right hand hovering above the mouth of the sack. The man was carrying a Val-Pack, an army officer's suitcase. It was heavy enough to pull him down on one side. He was in his sixties, wearing horn-rimmed glasses. He seemed oddly self-conscious.

Shayne touched the plunger lightly, his cigar cocked at a steep angle. The man approached at a plodding gait. He was clean-shaven, but there were ingrained dirt specks around his eyes. Several paces from Shayne he said, "Mr. Maguire?" and thrust the suitcase forward.

His voice, high and squeaky, confirmed what Shayne already knew: the shadowy Mr. A. had sent a substitute. Shayne reached for the suitcase, and at that instant he was struck a blow on the left shoulder. The detonator fell to the sidewalk. He pivoted on the ball of one foot, his brain registering automatically that he had been fired on from across the street.

The man in the new clothes started at him in horror. He dropped the suitcase and turned to run. Power was on the sidewalk a few paces ahead of him. He fired. The man tumbled to the sidewalk, hit in the knee.

Shayne went down, putting the truck between him and his hidden assailant. He still felt no pain in his shoulder, but he couldn't do anything with his left hand. He reached for the paper bag, realizing as he did so that someone was above him in the cab. The gear-shift shrieked. His outstretched fingers touched the handle of the plunger. He twitched it toward him and drew the detonator in against his body, doubling over on it to hold it steady. The truck jerked out from the curb, the wires tightened, and with a fierce contraction of his whole body Shayne jammed the plunger down.

The explosion blew out the side hatch. In an instant the entire cargo-space was a sheet of flame. Power was beside Shayne, trying to pull the detonator out of his hand. Shayne gripped it convulsively. A small wiry man burst out of the cab and leaped into a waiting car, which shot away.

"Mike, for Christ's sake! Let go."

Shayne came to one knee and shook him off. He caught a flicker of movement at an open second floor window in a brownstone. He knocked Power out of his way and started for the building at a shambling run, his left arm dangling. Tim Rourke jumped out of the bakery truck and ran toward him.

The downstairs door of the building was propped open. Shayne heard running footsteps above him as he started up the stairs. He was feeling pain now, but he plowed on. Each flight seemed steeper, more treacherous, worse lighted than the one before. His lungs were bursting as he pushed through the heavy door at the top of the final flight and emerged into blinding sunlight.

He checked himself abruptly. The tarred roof was studded with a pigeon shed and various vents and chimneys. This was the first in a row of three brownstones, and as Shayne's eyes adjusted he saw a man racing toward the stairwell of the third building. He looked back for an instant. Shayne recognized Szigetti.

Shayne had come as far as he was going. He stumbled to the low coping overlooking the street. The burning truck had moved just far enough from the curb so it blocked both lanes. It was almost directly beneath Shayne, and as he looked over the coping he could feel intense heat.

"Power!" he yelled. "Jamieson!"

Power was nowhere to be seen. Shayne yelled twice more. Then Power and Jamieson ran out onto the roof behind him.

"What, Mike?" Power demanded. "What?"

Looking down, Shayne saw Szigetti burst out of the front door of the other brownstone and set out toward Tenth Avenue at a fast walk without looking back.

"Too late now," Shayne said.

CHAPTER 16

"Hell, Mike," Tim Rourke said. "It was a long shot right from the jump. You told me so yourself. Long shots sometimes come in, but not all the time or they wouldn't be long shots. Excuse the lecture, but I don't like the way you're taking this, pal."

Rourke, Shayne and Power were in a narrow cell on the ground floor of a hospital called St. Luke's. Shayne was stripped to the waist, sitting on the edge of a high bed while a young Turkish doctor worked on the hole in his shoulder. It could have been worse. The shoulder bone had been nicked, and he would have to carry his arm in a sling while the ligaments grew together, but in three weeks he could be back playing golf, no more than a half dozen shots off his usual game. This off-the-cuff diagnosis came from an X-ray technician. As for the doctor, he apparently spoke no English beyond "Hurt?" and "OK."

Rourke went on, "But if we'd been able to swing it, what a story, what a story! As it is, I don't know how much they're going to let me write."

He looked at Power, who was hunting for an ashtray. Power tapped the ash from his cigar into the cuff of his pants.

"Maybe not too much, Tim, at present. That's the point about black operations: when they poop out, the best thing is to shut up and cut your losses. Mike, I know how you feel, coming this close. One thing we can say, we sure as hell tried! Even as it stands it's far from a total bust. Actually we've achieved quite a lot."

"How do you make that out?" Shayne said through set lips.

"We've got two members of the original stickup team, Billy Matthews and Tug Wynanski. It's just a question of time till we pick up the others."

"Who won't be able to tell you a thing," Shayne said.

"But we don't know that. Look at a few of the leads we've got. Who rented the girl's apartment? Who leased the house on Staten Island? When we develop Tim's movie film we'll have a good picture of the guy who tried to take off in the truck."

"One of the things you're telling me is that you don't have the girl?"

"No," Power said with regret. "Somebody got there first. She was gone and Brownie was gone. The Jetstar you told me about took off from LaGuardia at five-forty-five, probably with Michele and the banker aboard. If they're still on board when it lands in Lisbon, I'll be very much surprised. But we couldn't call on the Air Force to shoot them down, could we? And to get another piece of disappointing news out of the way—the number she called did turn out to be the Swiss bank on William Street. But you remember she asked for extension thirty-eight. There are only thirty-seven extensions."

"Big surprise," Shayne commented. "How about the character who was carrying the suitcase? I don't suppose he was anybody?"

"Nobody at all. He did it for ten dollars and a new suit. But you never know. Somebody had to hire him and clean him up and tell him what to do. He's here in the hospital and we're getting a statement from him now. And the whole Kraus angle is far from closed. What the hell, Mike, it's police work. I can see now we were hoping for the moon. I wanted to go off the force in a blaze of glory, but that's not the way the world's run. The trouble was, too many things had to synchronize. I think we made a mistake in setting the price that high. Perhaps at a lower figure they wouldn't have taken a chance they could put you out of action before you could work the detonator."

Shayne said nothing.

Power went on, "Now look at a few plusses. We'll harass that bank a little. We probably won't be able to close them up, but he can't use it again, either. We've cost him some money and some prestige. All the information we've picked up will go into the international files. One of these days we'll nab him. The girl's finished for anything important. From now on the French cops will stick to her like a burr. Mike, don't look so damn depressed. You know as well as I do that nobody wins them all."

"I don't have to like it when I lose," Shayne said.

Power stood up. "You'll be staying over, won't you, Mike? I want to buy you a drink when we're under less of a strain. I'll have word from Lisbon in the morning."

Shayne winced as the doctor tightened the bandage and taped it in place. "No, I might as well get back. If it's anything interesting, call me in Miami. I'm sorry it panned out this way." He forced a small grin. "Maybe I'll feel more human back on my home turf."

The two men shook hands. Power left.

Shayne said, "Time for my medication, Tim."

"Sure."

Rourke held out the bottle of cognac. The doctor glanced at him while he drank, but said nothing, perhaps not trusting his English.

"You didn't come out too bad," Rourke went on. "There was nothing in that suitcase but phonebooks, so there's no point in asking for ten percent of that. But the seventy-five hundred bucks in the Grand Central locker is yours. *I'd* like to earn seven and a half for three days' light, agreeable work, including time in the sack with a damn cute chick, unless I miss my guess. You *had* to sleep with her, didn't you? She had to think you were definitely her boy. It was an obligation, poor chap."

"Lay off."

"Come on, Mike! You didn't accomplish much, but neither did they! Those drugs were going to be incinerated anyway. You got a bullet in the shoulder, but I've never known a small thing like that to slow you down. Let's go out and tie one on. I have a tentative date with Terry Fox, and she can probably dig up a friend." He added, "I didn't mean that the way it sounded."

He grinned, but there was no answering grin from Shayne. The detective worked his injured arm into his shirt sleeve.

"Christ, Mike!" Rourke burst out. "That bullet could have landed six inches away from where it did, and you'd be dead! What's wrong with you? You ought to be celebrating!"

Shayne turned a burning look on his friend. Rourke said warily, "All right, forget I said it."

"By God, Tim, you've put your finger on it!"

"On what?" the reporter said suspiciously.

Shayne told the doctor impatiently, "Finish it up, will you, doc?" And to Rourke: "Don't you see? Power said everything had to synchronize. That was true for us, but it was true for them, too. Their timing had to be perfect. One guy walked up to me with the suitcase. A car turned the corner. I reached for the suitcase, the gun went off. Another guy jumped from the car into the cab of the truck. And it worked. There was only one thing wrong. *They didn't kill me.*"

"Don't look a gift horse in the mouth, Mike."

Shayne laughed happily. "The shooter was six inches off. A little better aim, and I couldn't have pushed that plunger, right? Right!"

"I'm surprised at you, Mike. It's easy to miss even at point-blank range with a handgun. That was a downward shot, the hardest there is."

Shayne pushed off the table. Pain stabbed him in the shoulder. He stood still to let the doctor fasten a sling around his neck.

"No, I didn't tell you about this guy," he said, his eyes alive. "He wouldn't miss unless somebody told him to miss. Szigetti—he's one of the best shots I've ever seen."

"On a range," Rourke said skeptically. "This was in combat."

"Tim, at that distance he could have put a slug through

my skull with both eyes shut, in the last stage of Parkinson's disease. They *wanted* me to push that plunger. They *wanted* that truck to burn."

"Mike, make sense."

The doctor knotted the sling at the back of Shayne's neck. "OK?"

"Yeah, yeah," Shayne said impatiently. "The truck was loaded with envelopes. They certainly looked real. I opened one of them, and the stuff inside certainly looked like heroin. But I didn't give myself a shot to see what effect it would have on me. For all I know, it could have been sugar or cornstarch. Let's go."

"Mike, you didn't notice the way that truck was burning. If you think you're going to rake around in the ashes and find anything, let me tell you—"

Shayne stuck a cigarette in his mouth and Rourke lit it for him. "I wish I knew Turkish. I'd like to tell the doctor I feel better."

"Funny," Rourke said. "I feel worse. Maybe you'll tell me what this is all about if I stay out from underfoot and keep feeding you drinks."

Shayne grinned at him. "You'll have to do more than that, Tim, if I'm right. You just saved me from making a very bad mistake. I don't know what I'd do without you."

"I wonder myself," the reporter said glumly. "Not often, though."

Rourke still had the use of the police Ford with the phone in the back seat. When they arrived in front of the Motor Shop, a heavy wrecker was pulling out with the great charred hulk of the Sanitation truck. Only one piece of fire apparatus was still there, a small traffic-control truck with a revolving beacon.

"Want me to tell them to wait so we can look it over for burned cornstarch?" Rourke said.

"We're not looking for cornstarch. We're looking for heroin."

"Why, obviously," Rourke said sarcastically. "A couple of tons, wasn't it? It must be around somewhere."

They found a place to park on Eleventh and waited till

the wreck was gone and traffic on the block had been allowed to return to normal. Shayne got out.

"I have to pick a lock, Tim. I'll need more than one hand."

"I don't know anything about picking locks."

"Then it's time you learned."

In front of the small door into the Motor Shop, Shayne handed the reporter his wallet and told him where to find his collection of picking equipment. Together, not without difficulty, they managed to force the lock. Inside, Rourke located the light switches and turned everything on.

"Let's see, two tons of heroin," he reminded himself. "Where would be a good place to start?"

"First we find a truck with a dented fender."

They started along the line of disabled vehicles. When they reached the end Rourke suggested, "Maybe they hammered it out?"

"There wasn't time," Shayne said. "Well, it's not the first hunch I ever had that didn't pay off. As Power says, we really have achieved quite a lot, about as much as you could stick in a bug's eye—Wait a minute."

One of the five-ton monsters had been pulled out on the floor. The front end was up on jacks and one of the wheels was off. The hood was up. A pad was thrown over the fender so the mechanic could lie on it while working on the motor. Shayne strode toward the truck and jerked off the pad.

There was a deep vertical dent underneath.

"Here it is, by God!"

Rourke helped him open the side hatch. "Yeah," Shayne said with satisfaction, seeing the cardboard cartons and the bundles of nine-by-twelve envelopes.

"I'm a genius!" Rourke exclaimed, performing a jerky little dance. "I thought I was saying you were lucky to be hit in the shoulder, not the head. What I *really* was saying was that we ought to hurry down here and look for a truck with a dented fender."

He reached in to pull out an envelope. Shayne said

sharply, "Leave it alone, Tim. Close the hatch. We've got to hurry."

His tone was urgent. Rourke gave him a single quick glance, then slammed the hatch and fastened the toggle bolts.

"Now I know what we do," he said. "We get a few dozen cops and wait for somebody to show up. Mike, I believe we're going to pull this out of the fire!"

Shayne's mind was racing. It was more of a steeplechase than a race on the flat—jumps, quick turns, hazards, then finally a hard fast run on level ground to the finish. He snapped his fingers.

"Didn't you say we're in a hurry?" Rourke asked.

"Damn right we're in a hurry. A lot to do. Can you start one of these trucks?"

"Yes-s," the reporter said without conviction, looking along the impressive lineup. "Maybe."

"OK, the first thing to do is find one that runs."

He started at one end while Rourke started at the other. The hardest part for Shayne was getting up in the cab. On his first try the door swung closed and dealt him a bad blow on his injured shoulder. Inside the cab, one arm was all he needed. The first truck failed to start at all. The second kept stalling. The third took hold at once, sounding healthy enough when he raced it in neutral. There was too much play in the brake pedal, which was probably the ailment that had brought it in.

Rourke was still trying to find the starting mechanism of the last truck in line. Shayne tapped the horn and his friend came running.

"Open the hatch," Shayne called down. "See what's inside."

In a moment Rourke called back, "Junk. I don't mean *that* kind of junk. Cans, broken bottles."

"Full?"

"Right to the top."

"OK. Here we go."

He put the truck in low and eased out of line, applying his brakes at the end of the arc. They were very soft. He shifted into reverse and backed toward the grease pit at the far end of the shop.

"Give me some help," he called to Rourke. "I want to get right to the edge of the pit."

Rourke ran past and began waving. Shayne allowed plenty of time to stop.

"Now lift the tailgate. Can you see where it unfastens?"

Rourke disappeared from sight. "You mean the whole back piece? I see a couple of clamps, but don't blame me if —" He jumped down. "Try it."

Shayne pulled a lever, and the conveyor started clanking. He shut that off and tried another. Slowly the enormous body began to tilt into dumping position.

"I only want to dump part of the load. Tell me when to stop."

Rourke moved back to the edge of the pit and gave him a hand signal. Again Shayne guessed wrong, and the upended body began to descend. He tried something else. There was a sudden roar behind him as the chewed-up rubbish cascaded into the pit.

"Stop!" Rourke shouted. "That's enough! That's too much!"

Shayne returned the lever to its previous position and lowered the body. Rourke fastened the tailgate while Shayne moved the truck back down the floor. He drew up beside the one with the front wheel missing.

"I'm beginning to get it," Rourke said. "It's the old razzle-dazzle. We switch trucks. But *why?*"

"Later," Shayne grunted.

The reporter had to do most of the work. He transferred fifteen cartons, piling them carefully on top of the trash so anyone opening the hatch for a quick look would see nothing but cartons. He located the missing wheel and put it back on. Then Shayne maneuvered that truck back into the gap in the line, the third from the far end. Returning to the other truck, the one with fifteen cartons of narcotics on top of its usual cargo, he moved it forward to occupy the exact space where the other truck had been.

"Now we take off a wheel."

Rourke jacked up the front end and with Shayne's help managed to start the nuts. He rolled the wheel into the parts office, where he had found the other. They raised the hood. Shayne dented the fender with a careful blow from a pry bar, then concealed the dent beneath the oily pad.

"They've got different serial numbers," Rourke pointed out.

"I didn't look for serial numbers when I picked out the other truck," Shayne said. "I looked for the dent. And that's what's bothering me. Now we've got two trucks with dented front fenders."

He had backed the narcotics truck as far behind the others as he dared, but the sharp dent in the fender still screamed for attention.

"Hide it with something?" Rourke suggested.

"No, get me a hammer."

The reporter scrambled away, meeting Shayne a moment later at the other truck with a heavy ball peen hammer. "I don't know about beating it out, Mike. That's body work. You'd have to take off the fender."

"Like this."

Shayne took the hammer. Holding it close to the head so he could swing it with one hand, he brought it down hard on the fender. The small dent disappeared in a larger one.

"Oh," Rourke said. "Like that. Let me."

Using both hands, he slammed the hammer down on the right fender, which until then had not been damaged. He swung again and again, until both fenders and the radiator grille were bashed in all the way across, as though the big truck had lost a decision to an even bigger one.

Shayne stopped him.

Rourke panted, "I'm glad you let me come along, Mike. That's the most enjoyable work I've done in years."

"That's the *only* work you've done in years," Shayne snorted.

Rourke put the hammer back while Shayne looked around carefully to see if they had left any signs of their visit besides the newly damaged front end of the narcotics truck.

144

"We probably left fingerprints," Rourke said, coming back.

"It's a longshot," Shayne said with a grin. "And I think you pointed out that longshots sometimes come in."

"That's not what I said. I said they almost always lose."

They snapped off the lights and returned to the Ford.

"You've only got that one arm," Rourke said. "And you know me, the less roughhousing I get involved in personally, the better. We need some reinforcements."

"Just what I was thinking," Shayne said. "Reach me the phone."

CHAPTER 17

The next morning at seven-fifteen, after an all-night vigil, Shayne was drinking coffee out of a soggy container and trying to keep his eyes open. His shoulder throbbed unpleasantly. The coffee was laced with cognac, but it tasted more of cardboard than of either cognac or coffee. He frequently had to stay awake all night when he was caught up in a case, but this was the least enjoyable way to do it, in the front seat of a car.

The deadline, he knew, must be approaching. The truck had to be out of the Motor Shop before the first mechanic arrived. Shayne had gone to considerable trouble to set this up, and he couldn't afford to miss it. Nevertheless his head kept falling forward. The music coming from the dashboard radio blurred in and out.

Suddenly he saw a man wearing the familiar green Sanitation Department uniform. He shook Tim Rourke's shoulder.

The reporter's long, disjointed body was jackknifed over the steering wheel. He looked around wildly and exclaimed, "Whose deal?"

"Wake up, Tim. We're about to move."

"You don't think I could sleep at a time like this, do you?" Rourke said indignantly. "How long till daylight?"

"Damn it, Tim, open your eyes. The sun's been up for hours. Have some lukewarm coffee."

Rourke took the container. He said suddenly, "Somebody's going in!"

"That's what I'm telling you."

They were still parked on Eleventh, pointing uptown. The man in the green uniform had reached the Motor Shop door. Shayne caught a glimpse of wraparound dark glasses and a full mustache as he looked around. Then he was inside.

"Seven-fifteen," Rourke said in surprise, looking at his watch. "As late as that. Maybe it's somebody coming to work early."

"When did you know an auto mechanic to come to work early?"

"I guess I went to sleep," Rourke said sheepishly. "Where is everybody?"

"Around. Let's see if they're all awake."

He turned off the music and picked up the police transmitter.

"Shayne," he said. "It's been a long night, but we're about to roll. The guy's inside now. It shouldn't take him more than two minutes to put on the wheel. Everybody check in, please."

Three other cars responded.

"Good," Shayne said. "He's going to be easy to follow, and let's not lose him."

Rourke slurped down the coffee, his eyes on the Motor Shop door. Then the taste of the stuff hit him.

"You call that lukewarm? I call it cold."

The overhead doors slid up. A big Sanitation truck with a dent in its left front fender rolled through and stopped while the driver got out and closed the door. Shayne described what was happening to the other cars. The Sanitation man climbed back into the cab and the truck turned east. Rourke started the motor. Shayne made him wait a full minute before letting him follow. By then they had a report from another car that the truck was approaching Tenth, apparently intending to continue across.

The four cars maintained a loose net around the big truck as it went downtown on Broadway. At Seventeenth Street, the driver jumped a light, skirted Union Square and headed back uptown on Fourth Avenue. Rourke's Ford was now a block ahead of him. Another stock Ford was a block behind. The two other cars were moving on parallel avenues, one on Madison, the other on Third. At Thirty-third Street, the car behind them reported, "He didn't take the underpass. Watch it."

Rourke slowed until the gap between the truck and the Ford was only half a block. Shayne adjusted the rearview mirror so he could see the truck without turning around. Its left-hand blinker was flashing.

"Left, Tim."

At Forty-second, where Grand Central and the Pan Am Building interrupt the uptown flow, Rourke turned. The light was green at Vanderbilt, and he went through. The truck had time to follow but instead it swung toward the curb in front of Grand Central. A steady flow of passengers from the early commuting trains was pouring through the main entrance.

Shayne said, "The one place in town where you can carry a suitcase and nobody sees you. Not bad."

The truck's faulty brakes failed to halt it in time, and it drifted up to kiss bumpers with a police car standing there. The cops in the front seat were from the Traffic Division and had nothing to do with Shayne. One of them yelled at the Sanitation driver before moving on.

"Leave the motor running?" Rourke asked.

"No, shut it off. This is as far as we go."

They got out. The Sanitation driver had shifted in his front seat to unlatch the door on the inner side. A woman came through the crowd and handed a suitcase up to him.

"Michele!" Rourke exclaimed. "If she went to Portugal, she had a fast trip."

"She didn't go to Portugal," Shayne said bleakly. "She should have, but she didn't."

They had a minute while the truck driver, alone in the high cab, opened the suitcase to see how much he was being paid. The Walk sign flashed, and Shayne and Rourke crossed Vanderbilt. Shayne was wishing he didn't have an arm in a sling. The other three cars had closed in and he had plenty of assistance for a change, but there were things he preferred to do himself.

The truck driver came out of the cab, bringing the suitcase with him. Another man in the same uniform took his place, to drive the truck away as soon as the transaction was completed. It was Szigetti, Shayne saw, finally getting his chance to show how well he could handle a heavy truck. He craned over in the seat to get the sign from Michele. She was standing at the curb, apparently waiting for the light to change so she could cross Forty-second—easily the loveliest girl in an area which has a high concentration of good-looking girls.

"And here's where it hits the fan," Rourke said in a low voice.

The Sanitation workman in the dark glasses opened the side hatch. Michele looked in. Frowning suddenly, she reached past the driver to move a carton, revealing the worthless trash behind it. Her lips moved. Shayne couldn't hear the words, but from the way she shaped them he thought she was probably speaking in French.

The man's dark glasses glinted. He pushed her aside and moved several more cartons. His back stiffened. He held that position for perhaps three seconds, during which he must have made a painful adjustment. Then he snatched up the suitcase and raced toward the entrance to Grand Central, running in the gutter, in the narrow space between the pedestrians and the moving cars. A man stepped out of the crowd, carrying the commuter's badge, a dispatch case and a copy of the *Times*. He held out an arm toward the running man as if to stop him with the folded newspaper, and fired twice.

The runner went down as though he had been tripped by a wire. His glasses flew off.

"It's Power!" Rourke exclaimed.

"Sure it's Power," Shayne snarled. "Who'd you expect?"

Michele grabbed the suitcase. With her usual deftness and grace she darted through the moving cars to her waiting convertible, parked on the other side of the street with the top down, the motor running. She flung the suitcase into the back seat.

Rourke called to Shayne as he ran to cut her off. She saw him coming. Her face glowed with excitement, which made her look like a girl in her teens.

"Darling! Get in!"

"You get out, baby," Shayne said as he reached the door. "We're starting over, with new rules."

Her eyes widened. She looked up toward the Sanitation truck and gave him a hard push. He went back into the path of a charging taxi. The driver hit his brakes and veered abruptly. A front fender bumped Shayne and knocked him to one knee. In the high squealing of brakes he didn't hear the shot. There was a look of amazement on Michele's face. She slumped across the wheel.

Szigetti, in the high cab, had had another difficult downward shot. This time, seeing Shayne holding the door of Michele's car, he had been shooting to kill. He had to lean far out, twisting. Michele had pushed Shayne at the exact instant Szigetti squeezed the trigger. The bullet caught her below the left breast.

Shayne came to his feet, his face a savage mask. Two narcotics agents had closed in on the car, but they stood out of his way as he swung over into the front seat without opening the door. He worked his right arm underneath Michele and laid her back gently against his injured shoulder. Her face and lips had lost their color.

"Darling, we almost—" she whispered.

Then Tim Rourke was beside the car. "Was she hit, Mike?" he demanded.

Her eyes left Shayne and swam toward Rourke. What she saw was the diamond dealer, Jake Melnick, who had apparently been robbed and slugged by Shayne in her presence three nights before. Something jumped in her face, as though she had been lightly flicked. Her eyes came back to Shayne, who returned her look unflinchingly.

"That's right," he said. "The whole time."

There was disbelief in her eyes. Then, without words,

150

moving only the corner of her mouth and a fraction of one eyebrow, she contrived to send him a complicated message. It told him that life sometimes played peculiar tricks, but she regretted nothing.

She moved her head so her cheek was against the back of his hand, and died before he could say anything more.

CHAPTER 18

The chief narcotics man, a rangy, outspoken individual named McIntosh, had begun to lose his temper with Shayne.

They were on the third floor of the huge incinerator at the foot of West Fifty-sixth Street in Manhattan. It was hot in the immense room. Two yellow Sanitation trucks were drawn up at the edge of a rectangular opening in the floor. One of the trucks had a vertical dent in its left front fender. Both front fenders and the grill of the other had been bashed in. The trucks were being unloaded through the side hatches. As each carton was brought out by Sanitation Department workmen, the nine-by-twelve envelopes it contained were shaken onto a folding table. A small army of uniformed cops from the Police Department's Property Division checked each envelope against duplicate lists before consigning it to the hole in the floor.

Shayne watched the envelopes flutter down a steep chute into the main incinerator, which occupied the whole of the first two floors. A fire burned there twenty-three hours a day. Each morning the grates were pulled and anything left unconsumed was loaded into scows for eventual dumping far at sea.

The marks on Shayne's face were deeply etched. At this point he trusted nobody. The final burning of the narcotics was something he had had to witness with his own eyes. He was holding a fresh bottle of brandy in a paper bag. He drank occasionally, without offering it to any of the men around him.

"If you want to tell us about it here instead of in an air-conditioned bar, it's OK with me," McIntosh said, mopping his face. "You're calling the shots. But let's get on with it, Shayne. We've got some tidying up to do."

"I'm not stopping you," Shayne said evenly.

Tim Rourke put in, "I know how you feel, Mike. But it's all new to these guys. Power kept the whole thing under his hat. They can't talk to me because I'm an innocent bystander. They can't talk to Power or Michele or Herman Kraus—they're all dead. Mr. A., if there actually is anybody called that, is out of the country."

"Did you say Mr. A.?" McIntosh said quickly. "Now listen, Shayne. Rourke's a reporter. This is going to be off the record."

Shayne turned on him. "Tim knows what to print and what not to print. He's no maiden."

"I can't print a story I don't understand," Rourke said. "Climb down, will you? That's not tap water you're drinking. You're one of the greatest drinkers I ever saw, but you can't put away a fifth of cognac in two hours without losing some of your edge. I want to phone this in before the wire services get it."

"Let me put it another way," McIntosh said. "We've seized a large sum in currency. I understand you had an agreement with Power which might seem to give you a claim on a certain percentage of that money. Power's no longer around. We're not obliged to honor the agreement, and we won't honor it unless you start cooperating. I have a well-deserved reputation for being very nasty when necessary."

Shayne told him what he could do with the percentage and his reputation.

Rourke exclaimed, "OK! She was a beautiful doll, and it's a shame she was hit! Do you think she'd rather go to jail for fifteen years? She was a hustler, Mike. She had no more moral sense than a flea. Be reasonable."

His friend looked around at him and he said hurriedly, "No, I'm wrong. She was really a victim of circumstances. But I've got to write this the way I see it. If you don't want

153

her to sound like a hustler, you'd better do some talking. Who started it? Did she or did Power?"

Shayne was beginning to feel himself unclench as the cognac took hold. Slowly and deliberately he took another long pull. Then, looking down the chute, feeling the heat on his face, he began to talk.

"Kraus started it. But he didn't know what he was starting. He wanted a certain girl, and he knew she wouldn't go out with him unless he could take her places she didn't otherwise go. He began selling drugs from the police stocks. It was a reasonably foolproof swindle. If an envelope says heroin, nobody's going to take it to the police lab to find out if it's really heroin. Kraus himself was the one who had to certify the envelopes before they were burned. Then Power found out about it, probably from stoolies. Kraus was an easy man to break, and Power got him to sign an undated confession. Then he broached the big idea. Why not turn this marginal operation into something that would really bring them both some money? Instead of faking just a few envelopes, why not fake them all? Kraus had to agree. He began working overtime. He began drinking and worrying. Meanwhile Power was looking for a buyer. Only somebody important could handle a deal this size. He put out feelers, and the feelers got through. But communication was all one way. The buyer contacted him, and naturally he was careful, because Power was an honest cop."

"Honest?" Rourke said.

"Will Gentry thought so. But Power was getting close to retirement, and he probably figured out long ago that one big coup would make many years of calculated honesty worthwhile. They set up a deal. I think the half-million figure was probably fairly constant all the way through. How much were they paying on this last switch, McIntosh? How much was in Michele's suitcase?"

"Half a million," the narcotics man said.

"Yeah. And Power didn't have much in the way of expenses. Then all at once Kraus conked out on him. Maybe cold feet, maybe he couldn't stand the idea of all that junk going back into circulation."

Shayne was beginning to be caught up in the explanation. He didn't pretend to understand Power, but he knew what the man had done, and that was enough.

"When I saw Power first, he looked like somebody who hadn't been getting enough sleep. All that work and planning, all those risky communications through unreliable channels, his last chance at important money—all down the drain because of one unimportant clerk. Kraus was essential. He was the man who had to make the certification. The next time the banker called, Power had to tell him the deal was off. The banker didn't care too much. He hadn't spent any of his own money yet. But it made a good story, and somehow it got through to Michele. And she had an idea. Did they need Kraus? Why not organize an old-fashioned stickup? It shouldn't be hard, with Power giving them the route and the schedule, and putting only two cops on the truck. But now they had to invest some capital and run a few minimum risks, and naturally they wouldn't pay Power the full five hundred G's. He'd be lucky to collect a fingerman's fee. He didn't like that. He was too adjusted to the idea of half a million. Not to mention the fact that it would be out in the open, and the publicity would be bad for his reputation. That's where I came in. With his own man in the gang, a man who would do what he told him, it wouldn't be hard to get possession of the truck after it was stolen, and again he'd have something to sell."

"How did he put it to you, Shayne?" McIntosh said.

"He appealed to my patriotism," Shayne said wryly. "He also showed me Michele's picture and offered me a fifty-thousand-buck fee. It was no problem to get in. Rourke can fill you in on all that—he had a part in it. It wasn't complicated when it was happening, but it gets complicated when you talk about it. The plan for the stickup was a damn good one. We followed it right up to the final step, and then instead of going downtown, I went uptown. I set the ransom at half a million. This was supposed to smoke out the banker, and I think it might have worked, too, if Power hadn't rung in another variation I didn't know about. I passed on a set of instructions about how I wanted them to hand over the money. By that time Power had the banker's phone number—he got it from Michele's phone. Power told him to pay no attention to my instructions, but to shoot me in the shoulder, being very careful not to kill me. I had to be able-bodied enough to set off a fire bomb and destroy the truck. Of course he'd already switched trucks. At the end of that little episode, the way it looked was that the drugs were burned and the case was closed. But Tim and I got to thinking."

"I got to thinking?" Rourke protested. "You got to thinking."

"Whoa," McIntosh said. "You can't expect me to believe that Power, all by himself—"

"It was set up long in advance," Shayne said. "This was the original switch, which he had had to drop when Kraus stopped cooperating. The envelopes were all prepared. He conned me into checking the cargo, so if there was any question, I could testify that the real truck had burned. I pulled out an envelope at random, and it really had to be at random. Whoever faked those envelopes had to be somebody with access to police files and materials, over a long period of time. It couldn't be done in a couple of hours or even a couple of days. Kraus had already been killed. That left Power as the only possibility. Switching the trucks was simple. Those trucks all look absolutely alike except for the serial number, and I had no reason to notice that. He may even have changed the number, I don't know. He had a key to the shop. I'd guess he slipped in the phony truck a couple of nights ago. There wouldn't be a worksheet on it, and anyway the mechanics take those jobs in rotation and they're way behind. Yesterday at four, when the shop closed, I was in a midtown motel waiting for a phone call. Power let himself in, switched trucks, put on a wheel and took off a wheel, switched spark plugs and put a dent in the fender. About a minute's work in all. I didn't get there till about twenty after."

McIntosh whistled softly. "Now tell me about the switch last night."

"It's just the old army game, McIntosh," Shayne said, "except that instead of using three walnut shells and a dried pea, we used five-ton Sanitation trucks. We took the real truck off the floor and put it in line. We took a fake truck out of line and put it on the floor."

Rourke said, "Do you mind if I say 'Yes but' at this point? I can see why Power switched trucks, so we'd think the real truck was burned. But why did *we* switch trucks? Why didn't we just let him pick up the real truck and drive it to Grand Central? We still would have had him just as cold."

"Put your mind on it," Shayne told him.

"I already have, and it baffles me. I think we went to a lot of trouble for nothing."

"Do you?" Shayne said bleakly. "We could have had him cold for selling heroin. We couldn't have touched him on Kraus's murder. He had to kill Kraus. Even if everything went off the way Power planned, there would have to be an investigation, and Kraus would be sure to talk. An experienced cop like Power could make a point-blank shooting look like a suicide. And who else had that confession to leave as a suicide note? Of course it had to be Power, but could we nail him for it? Not a prayer."

Some of the puzzlement had cleared out of Rourke's face. "Mike, you're a marvel. They looked in the hatch, and thought he was trying to sell them a load of nothing. And he'd been through too much for that money, so he picked it up and ran. Did you get the guy who shot him?" he asked McIntosh.

"We got him," the narcotics agent said.

"And this'll give you a lever," Shayne said. "People always talk more freely when they're trying to argue their way out of a murder rap."

"Thanks," McIntosh said, studying Shayne.

"You're welcome."

Rourke put in, "And what about this Mr. Adam or Adamowski or whatever his name is? Are you sure there is such a person?"

McIntosh's manner became more cautious. "We're not entirely sure. We've heard rumors."

"What about that Jetstar?" the reporter persisted. "I don't suppose he was on it?"

"Officially," McIntosh said, "I don't know what Jetstar you're talking about. Unofficially, because you and Shayne have done us a certain service, I might as well tell you that the Jetstar which cleared from LaGuardia yesterday afternoon made an emergency landing at Gibraltar before continuing to Lisbon. Needless to say, this is being followed up with the Gibraltar police, and something may come of it. Meanwhile, as long as he's still at large, I probably ought to warn you, Shayne, that you've made a dangerous enemy."

"So has he," Shayne said softly, and dropped the empty bottle into the chute that carried it down to the incinerator. "Tim, let's get back to Miami."

The shattering new bestseller

about a terrifying cop murder

and its bizarre aftermath

THE ONION FIELD

by Joseph Wambaugh

author of THE BLUE KNIGHT
and THE NEW CENTURIONS

A frighteningly true story of two young cops and
two young robbers whose separate destinies fatally
cross one March night in a deserted Los Angeles
onion field where a bizarre execution burgeons
into an equally bizarre aftermath—the longest,
most intricate court case in California history.

"A complex story of tragic proportions . . . more
ambitious than IN COLD BLOOD and equally
compelling."—The New York Times

A DELL BOOK $1.75

Thriller of the year!

LAST MAN
AT ARLINGTON

a novel by Joseph DiMona

A TOP JUSTICE DEPARTMENT OFFICIAL...

A SWINGING HOLLYWOOD DIRECTOR...

A BOOZING BEACH BUM...

A SOCIALITE NYMPHOMANIAC...

A CORRUPT CONGRESSMAN...

A HARDBITTEN FOOTBALL COACH...

What did these people have to do with the assassination of John F. Kennedy? And why were they now marked to die?

You will stay up far into the night to find out the answer. The answer you find will keep you awake even longer.

A DELL BOOK $1.75